Rita

The Laird o' Cockpen

Vol. II

Rita

The Laird o' Cockpen
Vol. II

ISBN/EAN: 9783337047665

Printed in Europe, USA, Canada, Australia, Japan

Cover: Foto ©Andreas Hilbeck / pixelio.de

More available books at **www.hansebooks.com**

THE LAIRD O' COCKPEN.

A Novel.

BY

"RITA,"

AUTHOR OF

"DAME DUDREN," "GRETCHEN," "DARBY AND JOAN,"
"SHEBA," ETC., ETC.

IN THREE VOLUMES.

VOL. II.

LONDON :

F. V. WHITE & CO.,

31, SOUTHAMPTON STREET, STRAND, W.C.

1891.

PRINTED BY
KELLY AND CO., GATE STREET, LINCOLN'S INN FIELDS,
AND KINGSTON-ON-THAMES.

CONTENTS.

———◆———

BOOK I.

THE LAIRD O' COCKPEN.

THE LAIRD O' COCKPEN.

CHAPTER XX.

" BELIEVING THE WORST.

" 'Tis not the frost that freezes fell,
　　Nor blawin' snaw's inclemencie,
'Tis not the cauld that makes me cry,
　　But my love's heart's grown cauld to me."

BELLA and I were sitting over the fire.
Grannie had gone to bed with a bad cold, and
my cousin and I had the little parlour to
ourselves.

A week had passed since the day I had
witnessed the Highland Games, since the
Laird had presented me with his plaid, since
Grannie, staid and proper as she was, had
decreed I might accept that gift without any
outrage to laws of propriety.

I had seen him once or twice since then,
but we had had no more confidential talks.

The weather had changed entirely for the
worse. Day after day the gloomy clouds
poured down their torrents of rain, only relieved by occasional wild gleams of sunshine
which would burst through the riven clouds
with a mocking promise they never fulfilled.
I scarcely left the house, for the chill I had
caught had left me weak and languid, and the
doctor Grannie called in declared I needed
the greatest care.

How good they were to me, those dear
Scotch folk! What tenderness and thought-
fulness, what coddling and comfort, what
petting and fussing there was over me. But
now Grannie was ill herself, and Bella had
come to stay with us and nurse her, and so
we had been sitting cosily by the bright
fire, after supper, chatting in disjointed lazy
fashion as we generally did, and without
the slightest inclination to go to bed, as
old Jean had suggested to us a few moments
before.

The steaming port-wine negus she had brought us was on the table. The firelight threw pleasant glints of brightness across the shadows. Bella leant back in the big comfortable arm-chair, and gave a sigh of content.

"If you had ever been one of a large family, Athole," she said, "you would appreciate the luxury of peace and quiet like this."

"I suppose," I said somewhat absently, "that one never does appreciate what one always has, or can have. It seems so. Now, I like brightness, life, animation about me. When everything is so quiet one cannot help thinking, and remembering."

"You're ower young for that," said Bella. "I wish you were not so grave and old-fashioned. Just for a wee whilie you seemed to brisk up and get quite bright and lightsome; but you've fallen back again, and your little face looks so white and weariful at times that I am quite sad to see it. You're not happy, Athole, and I could make a shrewd

18*

guess to say why, if you would not be angry with me."

Then—why or wherefore I cannot say, but quite suddenly—all my strength seemed to go from me. The hands lying loosely clasped on my lap began to tremble, and the trembling spread to my limbs and a sudden fear of myself came over me, that I should break down, that I should not be able to hide my sorrow and my suffering always; that others guessed, knew, pitied me. I half turned away. I stretched out my hand to take the glass of negus which old Jean always prepared for me, but even as I lifted the glass my hand fell shaking upon the table. A little hysterical laugh escaped me. " I believe," I said, " that I am growing nervous."

In a moment she had slipped down from her chair and was kneeling by me, her arms round my trembling figure, her kind, dear eyes gazing up to mine.

"Oh, Athole, dear wee cousin, why don't you be frank with me?—why don't you let me help you? Do you think I can't see the

change—that I don't know you're just breaking your heart for sake of that fickle, worth-
less, ne'er-do-weel? You've never been the
same since he went to Edinburgh."

I was silent. My heart beat with heavy,
laboured throbs. I felt weak and faint and
powerless. Perhaps she saw some change in
my face, for her eyes looked frightened and
she rose quickly.

"Drink this, dear," she said, holding the
warm spiced wine to my trembling lips. "It
will do you good. You look like a ghost."

I obeyed her, and the warm, stimulating
fluid seemed to put some life and strength
into me. I leant back in my chair. My
hands and lips were steady now.

"I—I am very foolish," I stammered.
"Don't mind me, Bella. I shall be all right
in a minute."

Tears were dangerously near my eyes, but
I would not give way. I put strong con-
straint upon myself. She stood there beside
me in sympathetic silence, only stroking my
hair with her firm white hand—the hand

whose very touch had always seemed to me
to mean strength, help, kindness.

"Now you are better," she said at last, and
drew me into her arms as she resumed her
seat in Grannie's capacious chair. "But, all
the same, this will not do, Athole. You came
here to gain health, not to lose it."

"I wonder," I said wearily, "if it is very
hard to die?"

She looked at me steadily for a moment.
"Do you wish to do it?" she asked.

"Yes," I answered. "I assure you, Bella,
I do not care to live. I don't seem to have
anything that gives me any interest or hold
on life. I am not one of those whose place is
missed, whose presence or absence makes
much difference; and—and—oh, Bella, I
think my heart is broken—my heart is
broken."

With a wild sob I clung to her, trembling
like a leaf, and with all self-restraint gone
from me.

"Hush, dearie, hush!" she said soothingly.
"You are tired and weak and unstrung, and I

know you have had a great trouble. You
were very brave over it. But it has hurt you.
Won't it make you easier to speak of it? You
know I love you dearly. Your confidence is
safe with me——"

"Oh, I know—I know," I sobbed. "But
how can I tell you?—how can I speak of it?
It is all over now, Bella. I have got to live
on and live through it, and—and trust to
time for forgetfulness."

"He—he made love to you, then, and you
believed him, after all I told you, Athole?"

"Yes, after all you told me, Bella. It was
very unwise."

"Poor little child—poor little cousin," she
said tenderly. "But perhaps it is not so bad
as you think. He may care. He seemed
very fond of you. I saw he was from the
first, and he may have been obliged to go
away in that sudden manner."

"Oh," I cried between my sobs, "it is not
that—it is not that! He wrote to me from
Edinburgh. Such a cold, cruel letter, Bella,
and I could see then so plainly it had only

been a passing fancy with him—but for me—
oh, it means so much to me, Bella. I—I
cannot forget!"

"You will, some day," she said. "You are
too good and true to waste your life on an
unworthy and unprincipled man."

"I suppose," I said wearily, "he is all you
say—all everyone says of him. But he *seemed*
so different, Bella."

"He was aye good at make-believe," said
my cousin, wrathfully. "They used to say he
boasted he could turn the head of any lass,
gentle or simple, after half-an-hour's talk with
her. He had just such a way with him."

Such a way with him! I thought of the
handsome face and the bright eyes, the
winning speech, the charm of look and
manner, and my heart echoed her words.
And I had been so ready to believe—so easy
to win!

"Have you heard," asked Bella presently,
"that Mrs. Dunleith has left 'The Rowans'
and gone to Edinburgh?"

I started involuntarily.

" To Edinburgh ! " I faltered.   " No—I did
not know."

My jealous fancy followed her—imagining
her reasons—supplying all details.   She had
gone to Edinburgh because *he* was there.   No
doubt he wished it, finding her infinitely more
alluring and interesting than a simple girl—a
girl whose fault had been that one inexcusable
fault of letting him win her too easily.

My tears dried, a hot flush of shame and
indignation sprang to my cheeks.   Pride
came to my aid at last.   Why should I fret
and make myself miserable for sake of one so
faithless ?

I slipped down from Bella's arms, and took
the low stool in front of the fire.

" Now," I said, leaning my head against
her knee, " I want you to tell me everything
bad that you know of Douglas Hay.   Every
story—every scandal—whatever you have
heard of him.   Don't keep anything back.   I
want to know the worst—the very worst.   It
may cure me.   I hope it will.   Don't be
afraid of hurting me, Bella.   I can bear it—

indeed I can—and perhaps it will ease this pain of heart. I seem to have borne it so long, and it hurts me—it hurts me!"

"Oh, my dear, my dear," said Bella sadly, "there will be no healing of that wound for many a long day. I know it well. And what can I say more than I have said from the first? I blame myself often that I let you meet him—but I suppose it was to be. I could not have prevented it. And this I will tell you, dear—I never saw Douglas so much in earnest before. That night—here—why the blindest person could not but notice that his eyes and ears and care were all for you. Still, he has always been fickle; I suppose it is his nature, and—shall I tell you something, Athole? I fancy—I have heard hints—that Mrs. Dunleith has some hold on him, and she is a woman of the world and you but a child in comparison, and perhaps it was owing to her he left so suddenly."

I shook my head. I remembered his letter. Every word of it burnt like flame in my memory. Over and over again I told myself there was no excuse for him—none. If he had loved me as I loved him, as he had sworn he loved me, he could not have been so cruel. He could not have left me in silence and suspense.

I knew then, better perhaps than I could confess to myself, that the worse I thought of Douglas Hay, the more resentful and hard I became, the better would it be for me.

I must forget him if ever I desired any peace of mind. But at that time I never expected I should accomplish the task save at the cost of all that made up life for me—perhaps even of that life itself.

The blow had gone cruelly home, the wound was very, very deep, and as yet I had lost even all belief in the consolation of Time, and the long vista of days and months that must be *lived* through looked very blank and very dark and very hopeless then.

Bella talked on and I listened, my heart heavy within me at every fresh proof of my lover's unworthiness. For though I sought for such proof and demanded it, it had power to hurt me more than I confessed.

Always—always—I seemed to see his face and the love-light in his eyes, and to hear his voice saying: "Can you not trust me, sweetheart, in spite of all?"

But it seemed to me that he had killed all faith in men and men's words for ever in my heart, and had left in it only the dull ache of ceaseless pain, and a passive acquiescence in what fate might bestow.

BOOK II.

CHAPTER I.

GOOD-BYE.

" Thou hast left me ever, Jamie,
   Thou hast left me ever;
Often hast thou vowed that death
   Only should us sever,
Now thou'st left thy lass for aye;
I maun see thee never, Jamie,
   I maun see thee never."

THE chill of Autumn was in the air, the mornings and evenings had grown very cold and bleak, and I was still in the Highlands, and likely to remain there for the rest of the year. My father had taken his pretty young wife to Egypt and the Holy Land, on a long tour, and I was to stay with Grannie till they returned. I acquiesced in the arrangement, as indeed I would have acquiesced in anything that took responsibility off my shoulders and left me in peace.

Everyone was kind and gentle and forbearing with me. My health was decidedly stronger; the warm salt baths, for which I went twice a week to Nairn, and the wholesome food and air, had done me a great deal of good, added to which the peace and rest and the unfailing tenderness which surrounded me as with an atmosphere of unobtrusive devotion, were inexpressibly soothing both to mind and body.

At the time I may not perhaps have fully realised how much I owed to them, but in after years how the memory came back to me, and how plainly I could read the unselfishness of all the love and care so freely lavished upon me.

We were very quiet in the little house at Craig Bank. Grannie was not strong, and I had no heart for gaiety, so we seldom entertained anyone except the Camerons or kindly Mrs. Macpherson.

Flora was now formally engaged to Alick. and they were to be married within a year or two at the outside.

Bella and I were still devoted friends, and a day rarely passed without our meeting. Kenneth had gone to Edinburgh and was not expected home till Christmas. As for the Laird, he had returned to his own domains for the shooting, and I heard and saw nothing of him.

The quiet days went on, and their quiet and their peace began to soothe some of my own unrest, and to blunt the sharpness of that passionate pain which at first had been so terribly hard to bear.

But there was nothing now of the old girlish wilfulness and gaiety and happy enjoyment of life that had at first made my experience of Scotland so pleasant and so novel a thing. I seemed to have grown years older in those few months. Almost unconsciously I found myself adopting many of the quaint words and phrases and mannerisms of the folk about me. That staidness and gravity which I had at first noticed as so remarkable a characteristic of both old and young, began to shadow my face and manner also.

The calm was somewhat depressing at times, and the gradual saddening of my spirits deepened and increased in the dreary Autumn weather.

I was almost a prisoner in the house, and it was not always easy to get away from haunting thoughts and painful memories.

Of Douglas Hay I had heard nothing more. If Kenneth had met him in Edinburgh he did not mention it, but they had never been very friendly towards one another, even in their school days at the Academy, and it was scarcely probable they would fraternize now.

One October day, a day the sun had selected to show himself once more, I went out for a walk by myself. It was rather an unusual occurrence, but Bella was engaged till the evening, and the fine weather would have tempted me from the house, even without Grannie's gentle insinuations as to "a bit walk" being beneficial.

Mechanically I took my way in the direction of Tom na Hurich. The sky was a soft misty grey, the crimson bramble leaves looked gorgeous in their Autumn bravery of colour. The dull golds and browns of the trees, and the purple glow of heather, told of the last efforts of Nature to clothe the dying year in beauty.

I walked on briskly till I came to the foot of the hill. The air and exercise seemed to have put life and warmth into me. I looked up at the winding road, and hesitated as to whether I should take it or not. Far up, I could see a funeral coach and a small train of mourners. The sight was melancholy and depressing, for shadows were settling down on the hill-top, and the glints of sunshine came more rarely as the afternoon slowly waned.

I had not been to the place since that memorable day when Douglas had confessed his love, and that memory swept over me suddenly, sharply, with the old pain and the old longing.

I turned abruptly away; I would not go up to the cemetery. Why should I attempt to recall that scene, or live over again that memory?

As I turned, I saw a figure on the road before me—a figure coming straight towards me in the soft grey light. Before I could collect my thoughts, or resolve on any course of action, it was close beside me. I heard my name pronounced by that one voice that had made and marred the music of my life. I saw before me—pale, dusty, worn—the figure and face of Douglas Hay.

I stood there silent and still, wondering whether he would speak—why he was here. I saw his face flush and then grow pale. Impulsively he stretched out his hand, then let it drop as I made no effort to take it.

"Athole," he said huskily, "won't you speak to me?"

But I could find no words. I could only stand there in dumb and frozen silence, looking at the changed and haggard face, wishing in some dull, half-unconscious way that my heart would not beat so painfully.

"I—I only came from Edinburgh this

morning," he went on in the same low, uneven tones. "No one knows I am here. I—I just wanted to look at the old place once more, and, if I said the truth, Athole, I hoped Fate might let me have a glimpse of you."

"Of me," I echoed, finding voice at last. "Surely I am the last person you would care to see?"

A deep, dark flush crept over his white face, and spread to the roots of the bright hair above his temples.

"I have no right to your forgiveness, I know. I behaved very badly, but I was mad with jealousy that night, and I knew I was standing in your way. I could not marry you—what had I to offer? and they were all speaking about the Laird, and I know he loved you. I thought I would go away and leave you free. You would soon forget, and as for myself—well, I had never found it hard to do *that*—but somehow, I was wrong this time, Athole. I haven't forgotten—I can't forget, and, on the spur of some mad impulse I came here. I thought only to see you,

19*

even afar off, would be some consolation—but you are changed, you are not the same Athole. I suppose you will never forgive me, never believe me? I can't blame you for it."

"It would be strange if you could," I said coldly and haughtily.

All my pride was up in arms. Did he think I was to be taken up and thrown aside as his whims dictated?

"You would never understand," he muttered. "I know I am only making matters worse, explanations seem so useless."

I drew back and looked at him steadily. "There is no need," I said, "for any; your absence and your letter were enough. I suppose it flattered your vanity to make such an easy conquest, but I was very young and very inexperienced; this has been a lesson to me."

"I always told you I was a bad lot," he said bitterly. "You may believe the worst of me that you can imagine. But I shall not trouble you again. I am leaving the country.

I have had an offer to go to Canada, and I start next week."

I felt cold and sick as I heard those words. Going away—so far—so terribly far—where no word or news of him could reach me. I tried to keep my face unchanged, but I fancy I did not succeed under the strain of that sad, regretful gaze.

"I—I hope you will like it—and be successful," I stammered at last.

His laugh, short and bitter, rang mockingly across the still, soft air. "That," he said, "is very likely, but it makes no matter to anyone. Only—only—Athole, if you would just once take my hand in yours; if you would but say, 'Douglas, I forgive you,' I could face the future with a better heart. God knows it's a sad one enough, but you would not believe that, now."

"Actions speak more truly than words," I answered, the pain at my own heart seeming to make me grow more hard and cold each moment. "And I need only ask you to look back at yours—to remember the way you have treated me—I, who loved you—trusted you—so entirely."

"I don't think you loved me so very much," he said, "at least, if you did, you are very unforgiving."

"Perhaps," I said. "That is my nature. You probably have nothing of that sort to complain of from Mrs. Dunleith."

He started. An angry light flashed from his eyes. "Why do you speak of her?" he asked stormily. "What have you heard?—what do you know?"

"I know that you could find time to make explanations and farewells to her," I said coldly, "while I was left without a word, a sign. I know that you had not been long in Edinburgh before she went there too. I wonder you do not marry her. She is rich and independent, and not — too young. Surely it would be better than going to Canada."

He drew a step nearer. His face white and set, his eyes burning.

"Do you know what you are saying?

Marry *her!* Thank you, no. Dora Dunleith
is not the sort of woman a man marries.
You don't mean to say you were ever jealous
for one single moment of her?"

"Jealous!" I said, with assumed indifference. "Oh, no. That implies love, does it
not, and you have argued, to your own satisfaction, that I have never loved you."

" No more you have, or you could not so
soon have forgotten. I—I suppose you are
going to marry the Laird? He has asked
you?"

"He has certainly done me that honour," I
said.

"And you have accepted—it is settled—
arranged—of course?"

"It is not settled yet," I answered coldly.
"But probably that is a mere question of
time."

Some demon of pride, anger, almost hatred,
entered my heart. For once I had it in
my power to hurt him, to deal back something of the pain and humiliation he had
dealt me.

The shattered faiths, the broken hopes, the hours of passionate despair, all clamoured now for vengeance, and if every word and look of mine could have been a weapon to stab him to the heart I would not have spared one.

I was no longer Athole Lindsay, the innocent, trusting girl, I was an indignant and embittered and humiliated woman. I had loved him so dearly—so dearly—counting the days so empty that had not brought sight or sound of him, living a very lifetime in those brief hours of joy and companionship— and now it was all dead—all over for ever— and his hand had dealt the blow in very idleness and heedlessness of the suffering it would bring.

No wonder indignation lent me courage. Come what might he should never know how much I had suffered, should read neither regret nor sorrow in my face. I could not believe him in earnest even though I read the change in his face—the sadness in his eyes.

A lesson once learnt as mine had been learnt is hard indeed to forget. All youth's hope and credulity could not come to my aid, or further his cause again.

He was silent for some time after those last words. I did not look at him. I busied myself in arranging some of the wild flowers and autumn berries I had plucked from the hedges.

Presently he turned to me.

"I hope you will be happy," he said. Then with a sneer, "Certainly he is rich, and can give a woman all she most cares for. That is more sensible than marrying for love. But now, as I have said all, and you I suppose have done the same, won't you do what I asked you? Give me a kind look and word to take across the seas—try to say, 'You have been very bad, Douglas, but I forgive you.'"

The blood rushed in a torrent to my face. For a moment my rage and indignation deprived me of speech.

At last I found voice.

"No," I cried firmly, "I will *not* say it, for I don't mean it! I never *could* mean it! And I am glad you are going away, very glad. I hope Fate will never let us meet again—for all the misery of my life began with you, and with you it will go."

"Thank you," he said, turning very white. "You are giving me a double burden, but my shoulders are broad, and I—I suppose I can bear it. I never thought you could be so hard — so unforgiving — but I deserve it, I know. Some day you may judge me more mercifully, and think I acted for the best."

"I have not the slightest doubt you have done so," I answered, coldly. "Only your wisdom came a little late in the day, did it not? It is a pity you did not possess or acknowledge it before we took that walk."

I looked up at the hill, which the soft, grey clouds were shrouding, the winding road and the white grave-stones looked faint and indistinct in the light of the waning autumn day.

His eyes followed mine.

"It was a mad impulse," he said, in a low, shaken voice, "I should not have told you. But, whatever you may think, Athole, I meant every word I said."

I laughed mockingly. I could not have helped it. I scarcely knew myself in this new phase of feeling. So bitter—so hard—so cold I seemed to have become.

"It is growing dark," I said. "I ought to be home, and really there is no need to prolong this interview. We have said all that is necessary. We have agreed that the past was a mistake. And now——"

I paused. I met his eyes—their pained, sad gaze—their dumb beseeching—but they did not soften me. He half extended his hand. "And now——" he echoed, "it is to be good-bye."

A lump rose in my throat. I turned aside, striving valiantly to keep back the threatening tears.

" Good-bye," I said at last, and then, relenting, laid my hand in his. I knew in that moment how my heart had hungered for that warm and tender clasp through all these weary months.

He dropped it abruptly and turned aside. He did not speak. He did not ask me again to say, " Douglas, I forgive you."

If he had——

CHAPTER II.

"Oh! woman lovely—woman fair,
    An angel form's fa'n to thy share
'Twad been o'er mickle to gie thee mair,
        I mean an angel mind."

"It is all over," I said, as I hurried home through the gathering dusk. "All over for ever! Well, I ought to be glad—I think I *am* glad. It could never have come to anything."

Yet, if I was so glad, why did that constant dimness blur the landscape? Why did my limbs so tremble—my heart so ache? Can one ever *quite* deceive oneself—try as one may? I think not.

The details of that scene stood out sharp and clear. I could see that haggard young face—those pleading eyes—but still a wild, wicked joy was in my heart. I had had my hour of triumph. I had not let him see what his treachery had cost me. To the last I had been cold, hard, relentless. He had not been able to carry away with him any soft or foolish memory of the girl whose love he had won so easily, and valued so lightly. I was glad of that

"And now," I told myself, "he will go away. We shall never meet again — and surely—surely in time I shall forget. One cannot be unhappy always."

I reached home to find an assemblage of Camerons there.

Grannie gently chided me for being out so late, the autumn mists were unhealthy for people whose lungs were not strong. I parried her scolding laughingly. My spirits seemed at fever point.

Kenneth came forth from a crowd of adoring womanhood. He had run up from Edinburgh to announce some success—some brilliant prospects for the future.

They were all going to stay to tea—there was noise, mirth — chatter. Hurriedly I joined in it all, wildly conscious of a dark hour in store for me, but determined not to brood on its advent.

Kenneth had much improved. He was more manly, more self-possessed. He was full of a scheme that had evidently been discussed between Bella and himself before I arrived. She had been invited on a visit to some mutual friends in Edinburgh, and I was included in the invitation.

"You must come," they both insisted. "You will enjoy seeing the town and having a little gaiety after being so quiet here."

"When do you go?" I asked, vaguely interested in the possibility of enjoyment.

"Next week. Monday, if possible," Kenneth said. "I have to return on that day, and I would like to take you both back with me."

"What does Grannie say?"

"We have not told her yet," said Bella. "But you know you can do just what you wish with her."

"I think I should like it," I said. I was

conscious of a vague restlessness and discontent, a desire to get away from here and all the memories connected with it. I had heard so much of Edinburgh—its beauty, its gaiety, its historical associations, its intellectual and artistic society. Yes, certainly I would like to go, and the necessity for a rapid decision on that point, seeing that this was Friday, was pleasantly exciting in my frame of mind.

We all set on to Grannie and argued and discussed the subject until she gave in, for at first she was strenuously opposed to the scheme, declaring I was not strong enough, and that they would not take care of me, and that I was unfit for any gay doing, or the fatigues of sight seeing. But I would hear none of those excuses, and combated objection so successfully that my cause was soon won.

We were all in brilliant spirits. We sang, danced, chattered, until quite a late hour for that quiet household. Uncle Jamie drank whisky toddy until I fairly wondered at the strength of his head, and the patience of his wife. He told us anecdotes by the score, and sang songs in the broadest Celtic dialect. He teazed Grannie with even more than his usual zest, and related stories of her pet ministers that, to say the least of them, were risky and irreverent. All the same, we laughed heartily at them and at his wicked delight in the dear old lady's discomfiture.

It was close upon midnight before we broke up and I found myself alone.

Wearied and spent, I threw myself on my bed, trying to remember the events of the day, but it only seemed as if between myself and all that had been, and all that I had loved and cared for with that glad delight which is brief as youth itself, I must roll a heavy stone of forgetfulness.

Athole Lindsay, as I had known her, lay buried beneath that stone. The Athole Lindsay who rose to face life, calm, cold— with all its poetry and romance crushed out for ever—was a very different person.

Whether wiser or better, let her history say.

* * * * *

One gets over a heart-break in time, I
suppose. I could not wear my heart on my
sleeve, could   not   let   the   little   world
that knew me know also that I had been
jilted, deceived, fooled, by an unworthy and
fickle lover. I rose up on the morning after
I had parted with Douglas Hay, braced and
nerved to bear the life that lay before me.

They say that a man with a morning head-
ache is a teetotaler for ever—in theory. In
like manner a heart deceived in the spring of
its first hopes and promises, is a heart for
ever distrustful—in theory.

I told myself I would never care for any
man again—never trust any man again. I
meant it then, most sincerely, and in a calm,
cool, and most prosaic frame of mind, I left
for Edinburgh. The peace and callousness
which had fallen on my troubled heart and
torturing memories was very grateful to me.
Here was rest at last, a cessation from pain
and self-torture and the frame of mind which
I had endured so long.

A week ago, the thought of going to Edinburgh would have thrilled me with excitement, the alternate agony and fear of meeting my false lover. Now—well, now I looked calmly out of the window as the train sped on over hill and moorland, and told myself it mattered nothing to me were he there or not, whether chance decreed for us another meeting, or whether he had already shaken the dust of his native land from off his feet, and gone to a new world and a new life which would part us for ever.

The journey did not fatigue me. It seemed full of interest, and Kenneth and Bella were excellent travelling companions.

We drove straight from the station to her friends', the Frasers. They lived in a large house overlooking one of the fashionable squares.

The bustling streets, the brilliant shops, the crowds of people, were exhilarating after the quietude of Inverness, and as we drove along I became more and more conscious that I had done wisely in coming here.

There would be no memories of the past to

20*

haunt me, no familiar road or walk to face my thoughts with that ever recurrent, "Here you came together," and with every effort of will, I resolved that I *would* enjoy, I *would* forget, I would "take the gifts the gods might send me," and put away from mind and memory that sad and painful time of shame and self-torture.

Surely it could not be so hard to forget. Surely life had good gifts laid up still. I looked at Bella's sunny face, at Kenneth's kind, grave eyes that so often sought my own, and at least, if my heart did not beat very gaily, its load seemed less heavy and less hard to bear.

Warm welcome awaited me. I was not allowed to feel myself a stranger for a single moment. Kenneth left us at the door, but was coming back later in the evening. Meanwhile, Bella and I were shown into a large and cosily-furnished bed-room, where firelight and lamplight made a glow of warmth and comfort, pleasant enough after the long, cold journey.

Tea was brought to us, and we removed our dusty travelling wraps, and, clad in warm dressing.gowns, sat with our feet on the fender, resting and enjoying the comfort of it all, until it was time to dress for dinner.

"Maggie Fraser said there were one or two people expected to-night," said my cousin, as we contemplated the evening dresses the neat Scotch maid was laying out for us. "What shall you wear, Athole?"

"Black velvet. It is too cold for light dresses." I said with a shiver.

"Isn't it rather—rather old?" asked Bella, dubiously.

She had elected to wear a pink silk gown, which, to my thinking, was far too bright and garish for her rather brilliant colouring and robust figure. But, as a rule, Scotch girls do not take kindly to quiet hues and subdued tints.

We dressed accordingly. I, in the plain black velvet, with its square-cut bodice and rich jet trimmings, unrelieved, save by some white flowers that the maid brought us—and

Bella, gay as any peony, in her pink silk and flowing train and flower-decked hair.

Thus attired we went downstairs as the bell sounded.

Everyone seemed already seated, or standing by the fire place in the drawing-room—a group, whose faces and figures were alike unfamiliar.

The usual introductions followed. Then, suddenly, unexpectedly, I saw among the faces, one looking coldly, scrutinizingly back to my own. I seemed to turn to ice—so cold, so strange a feeling took possession of me.

Before me, seated on a low ottoman, was a vision in palest grey, that floated, mist-like, about her graceful figure, and framed in soft folds the beautifully moulded neck and arms.

I was face to face with Mrs. Dunleith.

CHAPTER III.

"Oh, Nannie! the heart that is true
Has something more costly than gear;
Ilk e'en it has naething to rue,
Ilk morn it has naething to fear."

How poor and crude a thing seems youth before the finished graces and ready tact of a woman of the world.

Not by so much as the flicker of an eyelash did Mrs. Dunleith betray the smallest feeling, while I—I turned hot and cold, flushed and paled, and could scarcely summon self-command to bow, or return the conventional greetings of society.

For the sight of the woman recalled everything. My jealous fears, my self-torments, my lover's broken faith, my own doubts. And I read even in her one brief glance, that I was no stranger to her—that she knew something about me; perhaps Douglas had discussed me with her—perhaps they had laughed together over my foolish faith—my ready conquest!

With a great effort, I recalled my scattered wits, and tried to resume the composure that had been so easily disturbed.

Some grey-headed old gentleman was bowing to me, and offering his arm to take me in to dinner. I learned, later on, that he was a learned and celebrated professor at the University. I fear the poor man must have found me a terribly stupid and uninteresting companion. Try as I might, I could not keep my attention from wandering to that grey-gowned syren, with her soft voice, her low, sweet laugh, her indolent, graceful gestures.

The man who had taken her in to dinner seemed very devoted. He had eyes and ears for no one else. But, as far as I could judge, there was not much in her. She seldom spoke—and then only in brief response to her admirer's observations—but she was attentive and interested—I suppose men like that. Then she had so sweet a smile, so perfect a manner, that most of the women present seemed stiff, or coarse, or crude, by comparison.

I wondered not that the delicate flattery of such a woman's interest should charm any young man's senses—or old man's either, for the matter of that.

The fortunate—or unfortunate—individual, on whom she was practising her arts was decidedly middle-aged—almost as old I fancy as my own professor. But he seemed charmed and interested, which my friend certainly did not. After a time he gave up conversation, and devoted himself to his dinner—only addressing an occasional word to me now and then, respecting the merits of some dish I had refused.

But I had no appetite, and the dinner seemed to me a very long and wearisome ceremony. Like all things however—be they bad or good—it came to an end at last; and the silks and velvets rustled away into the drawing-room, and I found myself once more under Bella's wing.

Scarcely had we seated ourselves, however, when Mrs. Dunleith dropped, in graceful languor, into the low settee by my side. She commenced to talk to Bella. I, most assuredly, was not inclined to further, or commence conversation.

They discussed dresses — the Northern Meetings — Highland scenery, and various other subjects. She told us that she intended returning shortly to the Rowans. "Indeed," she added, glancing at me, "I had not intended to stay so long in Edinburgh as I have done. I merely came on a matter of business—to assist a friend in whom I take an interest—a very great interest. I am happy to say I have been of some service to him ; but he is leaving Scotland next week, and then I shall go back to my little house again."

I was silent—but the hot blood burnt in my cheeks, and a feeling of bitter indignation swelled in my heart. Well enough I knew who was the friend in whom she took " a very great interest." So it was through her influence Douglas Hay had secured this appointment in Canada—that he was about to leave the country.

Well, it did not matter now. Whether he was in this land or any other could make no difference to me—only a spasm of jealous agony contracted my heart as I thought how she had come between us—for some instinct told me that, no doubt, she had warned him against the folly of early engagements—or worked on his feelings until they seemed selfish and inconsiderate. She had parted us with her sweet voice—her pretended sympathy—her charms and witcheries—beside which, I felt my youth and bluntness and inexperience made but a poor show.

And now she was sitting there—stabbing me with every word and hint, and graceful languorous glance. She, who could do what all my love had been unable to do.

I wonder how it is a woman guesses she has met a rival ?

Mrs. Dunleith and I had never interchanged

a word with one another before this night.
Yet we both seemed to recognise that we had
cared for the same man. I say "had cared,"
but, probably, she cared still. I fancied so,
and I almost wondered she had not tried to
win him more securely. Surely it could not
have been so very difficult for one who had
done so much.

I had yet to learn, however, that Douglas,
if malleable up to a certain point, could be
iron and adamant beyond. He had left himself in this woman's hands with the careless-
ness and conceit of youth. He knew she
cared for him, but—though I only learnt this
long afterwards—he did not care for her in
like manner.

He pulled himself up, short and sharp, just
as she fancied she was leading him where she
desired. I might not have believed this then
—even on her own confession—but the day
was coming when I should learn more of
men's ways and feelings, and judge them less
harshly, even if I thought of them less
highly.

It was a relief when Kenneth entered, and at once joined us. Then the other men came in from the dining-room, and we broke up into groups of twos and threes, and music and conversation filled up the rest of the evening.

"I hope you will enjoy yourself here," said Kenneth, as he bade me good-night later on. "I shall come and take you about as much as possible. You have been rather moped at Grannie's. A little amusement and excitement will do you good."

I agreed that it would. I had determined to throw myself heart and soul into everything that was pleasureable and gay. Surely that would cure this dull ache—this constant memory.

I was so tired that night that I could scarcely speak to Bella, and in two minutes after my head touched the pillow I was sound asleep.

* * * * *

Clear air, a bright sky, noise, bustle, exhilaration. I woke to all this and prepared, with a lighter heart than I had known for many a long day, to explore the city. Kenneth was our guide, and we drove of course through Princess Street, and viewed Scott's gigantic monument and the beautiful public gardens, and the famous Castle, and walked through the old town, and went up to Arthur's Seat, and then returned tired—but by no means half sated with sight-seeing—for luncheon.

To my inexpressible amazement who should drop in at luncheon-time, with all the *savoir faire* of an old and welcome friend, but the Laird of Corriemoor. He explained he was in Edinburgh on business for a week or two, and as the Frasers were very old friends he naturally came to see them at once.

Bella looked mischievously at me as she listened to his elaborate explanations. It was plain that she at all events, did not credit him with absolute truthfulness in the matter.

The Frasers were, however, quite unsuspicious, and if I felt a little embarrassed and surprised at first, I hope I did not show it very plainly. Bella assured me I did not, so I was comforted, and put the best face on the matter.

I must candidly say that whatever business had brought the Laird to the city, he did not spend very much time over it. He was constantly with us, greatly to Kenneth's annoyance. He took us to theatres, museums, and accompanied us on drives, walks, and excursions of all kinds.

I cannot but say I enjoyed it all. He was so well-informed and clever that all matters of history, archæology and literature connected with Scotland, became both interesting and intelligible to me.

He seemed to know every house and history of the old town, and every story and legend of famous Holyrood. We spent hours there, and the sorrow and the pathos of its many memories acquired a painful and vivid interest for me. No longer could I say that I had little knowledge and less interest in Scotland, and things Scotch. With such a guide and companion that confession would have been rank heresy. Quiet and grave as the Laird of Corriemoor seemed on first ac- quaintance, it was marvellous how he unbent after a time, and how genial and pleasant a companion he could make himself.

Scarcely a day passed that we did not meet. Indeed I had grown so used to his appearance and escort that I should have felt quite strange without them. Bella wisely kept silence, and for the space of three weeks matters went on as I have described.

Mrs. Dunleith had gone back to Inver- ness. That fact said plainly to me that Douglas Hay had taken his departure also. I had not seen him since we parted at *Tom-na-Hurich*, nor heard word or news of him.

It could not matter. I told myself that silence was best, and its sombre veil fell darkly between my lover and me.

A change, a subtle, indefinable change, had come over my feelings and myself. Whether I was the happier or the better for it I could not say, but at least I had a brief space of rest and peace, and I told myself that it would last always—always now.

* * * * *

"Bella," I said, coming abruptly into the bedroom one evening, where my cousin was comfortably ensconced in an arm-chair and luxuriously busy in doing nothing, except looking at the fire—"Bella, I have some news for you."

She raised her merry dark eyes to my face. "Are you sure," she said, "that it will be—news?"

"It ought to be," I said. "I only made up my mind half-an-hour ago. I am going to marry the Laird."

"Of course," she said coolly, "I always knew you would."

I sank down in the companion arm-chair to her own, and looked at her with indignant unbelief.

"I am sure you did not," I said. "You couldn't have known it. No one could. Nothing was further from my intentions. I never *dreamt* of such a thing when I came here."

"Probably not," answered Bella; "but, dreaming or waking, one could see what it was all tending to. And indeed, dear," she added gravely, "I am very—very glad. He is so good, and the marriage is altogether so suitable, and certainly he has been most devoted ever since he saw you first."

I laughed somewhat hysterically.

"Well, this was the third time of asking," I said. "He has certainly displayed his national virtue of perseverance."

"How did he do it?" asked Bella laughing. "Somehow I *cannot* fancy the Laird making love."

"Well, he did not follow the example of his countryman in Dean Ramsay's 'Reminiscences,' and allure me to a churchyard to say 'My folk lie there; wad ye no like to lie there wi' them?' His three proposals have all been very matter-of-fact. I——"

"I am glad of that. I hope he won't 'make love' as you call it."

"Don't you think he is too sensible, and—well—and too old for that, Bella?"

"As to being sensible," said Bella, "don't they say love makes the wisest man the biggest fool? and as for age, I won't be sure that the Laird is so very old, my dear, not more than seven or eight-and-thirty. That's not old for a man."

I was silent, gazing meditatively into the fire and twisting absently round and round my finger the ring that had been so recently placed there, just to keep me in mind of him, my affianced had said. On the morrow he was to bring me another one.

"No," I said at last, "I suppose not; but it seems old, Bella. I am only seventeen."

"Have you quite made up your mind?" she asked gravely. "Do you think you have got over that—that other? That you have really forgotten——"

"I am quite sure," I said slowly, though a strange tightness seemed about my heart, and a lump rose to my throat and impeded my speech. "I do not say I have forgotten, but

21*

I have ceased to care. I have got over that fancy at last."

Bella looked at me somewhat anxiously. "I hope—oh, I hope you are not deceiving yourself, Athole," she said. "You may make two lives unhappy instead of one, and after all, do yourself no good. I suppose you don't care very much for Donald Campbell?"

I was silent for a moment, trying to face the question honestly and fairly as I knew it ought to be faced.

"I care for him enough to marry him," I said at last. "I know there is no romance about it, but that is all the better. Most married people, as far as I can judge, get heartily sick of one another in a year or two. I suppose it comes from expecting too much, and all that glorified ideality which means love, and is as unreal as—well—as love. I have done with all that nonsense. I have learnt my lesson, and now I am going to profit by it. We shall be a sensible, matter-of-fact pair, neither of us expecting too much

or exacting too much from the other. We
ought to be happy."

Bella shook her head. Her bright eyes
looked a little dim and saddened as I met
their loving gaze.

"Ah, my dear," she said, "those senti-
ments would sound very well if you were
thirty-seven instead of seventeen. As it is I
know you neither feel nor believe them. Be
honest and say so."

I only shook my head. "Indeed, Bella, I
do mean them. I have grown much older
and more sensible in these last few weeks,
and I like him very much. I really do. He
is so good and kind, and he seems so *true*.
After all that is the best thing to trust to.
Better than romance or love. And you
know I am not wanted at home. Since
papa married again he does not seem to
care for me as he used to do, and Eleanor is
so jealous. I suppose she wants to have him
all to herself. Well, I will not interfere with
them any more. It seems funny,"—and I
laughed, but not very mirthfully I fear—

" to think that I shall be able to invite them to stay with me, to offer them Highland hospitality—fishing, shooting, all that sort of thing. By the way, what kind of place is Corriemoor ? "

" I have never seen it," answered Bella. " But I have always heard it is a very fine place, and very large, miles and miles of moorland—lochs for fishing, and shooting wild birds — grand scenery — beautiful air. Oh, I'm sure it is a very fine place, indeed. But how will you like the Laird's mother, I wonder ? You know she lives with him to keep house for him. But perhaps she will leave when you go there."

" She is welcome to stay," I answered with indifference. " I am sure I shall not interfere with her. And as I am quite ignorant of housekeeping I shall be very glad to have her."

I rose from my chair and Bella did the same.

Suddenly she drew me into her arms, as tenderly as a mother might have done.

"God bless you, poor wee bairn," she said softly, "and give you strength and make the path easy for your feet. I cannot say that I'm altogether happy about you, though you've acted wisely, and he's a good man, and loves you dearly, I'm sure. Still——"

My kiss stayed the words on her lips, and they ended in a sigh.

CHAPTER IV.

" Lilies for a bridal bed,
  Roses for a matron's head,
  Violets for a maiden dead,
    Pansies let my flowers be :
  On the living grave I bear,
  Scatter them without a tear,
  Let no friend, however dear,
    Waste one hope—one fear for me ! "

So it was all settled, and I had sealed my fate.

Everyone seemed pleased who heard the news, and congratulations poured in on all sides. Everyone—that is to say, with the exception of Kenneth. He neither looked pleased, nor expressed satisfaction. However, I fear I paid little heed to him, I was too engrossed with the new responsibilities and exigencies of my position as a betrothed maiden.

Grannie wrote rapturously on the subject,

and declared I must be married from her house. We all seemed to take my father's consent for granted—but really there could be no possible objection to such a son-in-law as the Laird of Corriemoor, and I had not the slightest doubt he would only be too grateful to the man who would take me off his hands and leave him free to be the slave and worshipper of his newly-wedded and most exacting young wife.

My lover was not a very passionate, or ardent one. He evidently liked to be with me. He was most generous in gifts and offerings, but he did not attempt that performance of which I had expressed such a nervous dread, viz., " making love."

I was not of a demonstrative nature myself. It had never been easy to me to express my feelings. I had none of the pretty provocative caressing ways of most women, and it would have been a sheer impossibility for me to have coquetted with, or teased my grave, staid lover, even had I wished to do so.

He took me for walks and drives as of old, but I still had Bella with me, and he never made the slightest objection to her company.

At the end of a fortnight he hinted that he must leave Edinburgh and betake himself to his ancestral halls, there to break the news to his mother.

" It is more respectful to do so by word of mouth," he said, and I agreed, with due deference and a vague expression of regret at his absence, which I am afraid I did not really experience.

My visit to Edinburgh was drawing to a close, so Bella and I returned under his escort, and after spending one night in Inverness he left for Corriemoor, and I settled down to the old quiet life, which lasted with but little variation until the arrival of my father's letter.

It came from Cairo, where they were staying, and as I expected gave glad and gracious sanction to the proposal of any individual rash and generous enough to relieve a father of the expense and responsibility of a feminine dependant.

It is a daughter's duty to get married—
well, if possible, but at all events to get
married. Probably he had not hoped or
expected such a speedy or gratifying result
from my visit to his native land. Of course
he knew Corriemoor well, and the Campbells
of Corriemoor were as a household word in
the family. He would not be back in
England for six months, but there was no
need to wait for his presence, if the bridegroom was impatient and the bride acqui-
escent. He enclosed a cheque for £200 for
the trousseau, and referred the Laird to his
lawyers for all particulars as to his affairs and
my prospective inheritance, announced that
Eleanor joined with him in love and good
wishes, and they both trusted that I might
be very happy—as happy as they were themselves.

That was all. Grannie and I read it, and
then I sent it on to the Laird, with an
enclosure for himself. He was quite satisfied,

and wrote back proposing that we should be married as soon after the New Year as I could decide upon.

I looked apprehensively at Grannie, as I handed her the letter containing the suggestion.

" It is so soon," I said.

" 'Tis ill waiting when the will is gude," laughed the old lady. " Take him, my bairn, and don't ask for delays. You'll aye be the better for settling down and getting acquainted with one another, and no courting will teach ye that, take an auld woman's word for it. Ye may see each other every day and all day, but it's no' the same as one good week of steady matrimony. Lovers are aye on their guard, but husbands and wives know that they must just put up wi' their bargain, and if it is so based first on solid virtues, and good honest love and respect, there's nae much to fear of results."

Wise words, good sound doctrines, Grannie. A pity they sounded so cold and commonplace to me.

While December was yet in its early days
the Laird returned, and the question of our
speedy marriage was again mooted.   I let
them arrange it as they pleased, so the middle
of January was fixed upon for the all-im-
portant ceremony, and I was engulfed in a
whirl of millinery and haberdashery which
was a very novel sensation, and appeared to
offer endless gratification and excitement to
Grannie and my cousins.

My future mother-in-law sent me a kindly
though somewhat formal letter of congratu-
lation and welcome. She regretted her health
would not permit of the long journey to
Inverness in the winter-time, but looked
forward to welcoming me at Corriemoor as
her daughter when our honeymoon was over.

Our honeymoon!

The words seemed to appal me as I
read them, standing out in that clear firm
writing.

My spirits fell as they had not fallen yet.
A honeymoon—a whole long, weary, dreary
month to be spent in uninterrupted companion-

ship with just one man. No merry feminine
chatting crew to laugh and jest with—no
friends to visit or receive. Only he and I
together—husband and wife—yoked for life
in matrimonial harness, to make the best or
worst of our experiment.

For one wicked unholy moment my
thoughts flew to Douglas. There would have
been no hardship in such a prospect had he
occupied the place of bridegroom—but the
Laird . . . . what could we say—what
could we do that would make the time less
wearisome and monotonous? And in the
winter—the cold dreary days when rain or
snow might keep us chained to the dreary
grandeur of hotels! Ugh! I shuddered as I
thought of it.

A sudden resolution took possession of me.
With the letter in my hand, I marched off to
the drawing-room, where my affianced was
awaiting my tardy presence.

"Laird," I said abruptly—having yet
vainly tried to accustom my tongue to more
familiar greeting—"where are we going when

we're married ? Do you want to stay here—in Scotland ? "

He turned his ruddy, weather-beaten face to me in some surprise at my unexpected question.

" I had thought of taking you to Perth. It is a bonnie town," he said, with some hesitation. " I fear the weather will be somewhat inclement for the Lochs, or we might have gone to the Western Islands. But, my dear, it is for you to say. Where would you like to go yourself? Just say the word, and I'm not likely to deny you."

" I should like to go away from Scotland altogether," I said. " It is so cold, so bleak, so dreary. Can't we go abroad—say to the South of France, the Riviera, anywhere where we could find blue sky and sunshine ? I feel frozen up here."

" Go abroad ! " he repeated — genuine consternation visible in every line of his face. " Away—out of the country ? Is that what you mean ? "

" Yes," I said. " To some warm country

I know you have never been out of Scotland, but that will make it all the more interesting. I'll do all the talking, if you can't speak French or German."

He sighed hopelessly.

"You shall do just as you please, Athole," he said, with creditable meekness. "I suppose Scotland is somewhat bleak and cold for a delicate wee thing like yourself. But remember, my dear, I know nothing of foreign ways and customs, and fear I shall aye be blundering and bothering you. Will you put up with that?"

"Oh, yes," I said laughing, and too pleased at my easy triumph to cavil at anything else. "Don't be afraid, Laird, we shall get on very well, and it will be great fun to see how surprised you will be at the difference between foreign customs, and your national ones."

He smiled a little sadly. Perhaps he did not think his honeymoon a cheerful prospect, or see the "fun" that his unfamiliarity with things new and strange and incomprehensible might afford me, in quite the same light as I did.

However, it was arranged that we should journey into foreign lands in search of warmth and sunlight, and the excitement of making plans and deciding upon different routes greatly relieved the usual monotony of our daily interviews.

I had always had a great desire to go to Nice and Cannes, and see the lovely blue Mediterranean, and revel amidst the palms and orange groves, when less favoured folk were shivering over fires and fogs at home.

I hated cold. Warmth, brightness, sunshine, were like life to me, and the vision of a Scotch winter in the lonely wilderness of Corriemoor had simply appalled me.

But I had triumphed. Whatever the Laird really thought, he affected, "a virtue though he had it not." He seemed pleased and contented, and I was willing to believe he really felt so.

Meanwhile the days seemed to race along.

The last remaining week of maiden liberty already announced itself.

We had kept the New Year with wassail and merriment, and much feasting, and my relations and friends had vied with each other in the giving of dinners and suppers and such like festivals in honour of my prospective bridegroom and myself.

I was growing a little tired of it all. Of the speeches that were almost always the same, the solemn ceremony of eating and drinking that invariably lapsed into orgies when ladies withdrew, and whisky appeared, and the revellers emptied the "flowing bowl" to our health with more goodwill than discretion. There certainly was a good deal of similarity in all these entertainments, and I now and then had serious doubts as to whether even my grave and strong-headed Donald was altogether circumspect in the matter of potations.

I supposed, however, it was the custom of the country—though for the life of me I could not see why people should drink more than was good for them, and incur the penalties and discomforts arising therefrom, in order to show their appreciation of a fellow mortal's matrimonial bliss.

But the national beverage—with or without excuse—was ever flowing in generous streams, and all sorts and conditions of men partook of it—and were the result of it. I did not like the custom, I must say, and I thought it a singular fact that so religious and Bible-quoting a race, should be also such an inebriated one.

But the Scotch have their own way of interpreting the Scriptures, and I am not sure that they could not find or twist a host of texts to mean that whisky-drinking was a matter altogether pleasing to the Almighty, and specially demanded as a duty of His elect! I wondered could they picture Heaven without it!

＊　　　＊　　　＊　　　＊　　　＊

My wedding day dawned clear and cold, with a steely sky and faint gleams of sunshine.

22*

In accordance with Scotch habits, I was to be married in the house.

Bella assisted at the important function of the toilet, which was simplicity itself.

"If only you were not so pale," she said, as she fastened the snowy veil which covered me from head to foot.

I looked at myself with a strange sense of unrecognition. So small, so white, with such wistful dark eyes, such tremulous pale lips— surely this was not how a happy bride should look. But was I happy?

For a moment the thought flashed across me—keen in its pain and regret. The face that looked back at me was the face of one who had abandoned all hope, and lost all joy.

For the first time it seemed to me that I was acting both wrongly and unwisely. I was marrying a man for whom I cared but little—if at all—certainly not as a wife should care for her husband.

Certainly I had made no false professions— I had never told him I loved him—but perhaps he had taken that for granted. The full importance and solemnity of my action impressed me at last. Until this moment, when I stood and looked at that small white figure, and that young sad face, and knew them for my own, on this my bridal day, I had not fully realized what I was taking upon myself.

I shuddered and turned aside, and for one brief moment my self-command trembled in the balance.

Bella took my hands, a look of alarm in her eyes.

"Hush, Athole. Oh, my dear, you mustn't break down—not now."

I snatched my hands from her grasp, and pressed them tight against my eyes, trying to keep back the tears that threatened to break forth. I shook from head to foot, but I would not give way to the hysterical emotion that had seized me.

It was so foolish, so weak, and ah! so useless now.

"Don't speak, Bella, just leave me quiet for a moment," I entreated, and with ready tact and good sense she turned away and stood by the window, waiting till I had recovered my self-control.

Presently I turned to her, and held out my hand. "I am—quite ready. Let us go down," I said.

My voice was quite steady. She looked at me. I saw her eyes grow suddenly dim. But mine were dry and tearless now.

CHAPTER V.

" And you must love him, ere to you
    He will seem worthy of your love."

" And often, glad no more,
        We wear a face of joy because
    We have been glad of yore."

" A man he seems of cheerful yesterdays
    And confident to-morrows."

WHAT a long time since there have been any entries in my diary!

Sometimes I have thought I would give up the foolish habit altogether. There is no use in being confidential to paper and ink, and it is but a poor satisfaction to see the record of one's follies and errors and griefs staring one in the face after a lapse of time.

Yet habit is strong, and they say women must always have *one* confidante. I have none save this book with its pages, some blank, some full, and certainly I can be more confidential to it than to any human being, so to-day I open it again, and make the first entry I have cared to make since my marriage.

My marriage!

Surely it was years and years ago that I stood in the little drawing-room at Craig Bank, and, surrounded by admiring relatives and friends, put my hand into the hand of Donald Campbell and heard the simple words that made us man and wife.

And now, here we are, amidst bright sunshine and blue seas, and the prospect on which I look is fair enough to delight any eye—poet's, or artist's, or ordinary mortal's.

The wind shakes the odours from the orange buds, the olive woods are silver-grey in the sunlight. It is a day early in February, but on this fair coast it might have been the height of Spring time, so sweet and mild is the air, with the breath of narcissus, and primroses, and myrtles, and violets, that blossom by millions under the sea-terraces, and in the woods of the villas.

The hotel windows look out on the blue Mediterranean; the sky is rose and gold in the west, where the sun is slowly sinking behind hills of amethyst, and snows of silver. All along the curves of the bay the sea flashes and sparkles as if glad of its own beauty—purple here, azure there, as the light catches its rippling surface.

Figures pass to and fro under the palms, the marbles of the Casino are white as snow in the lovely glowing light. Monaco frowns darkly from the crest of its rocky hill—white sails of yachts and pleasure-boats are drifting to Villefranche, or San Remo. I look at it all and think how beautiful it is, after the grey skies and chill mists and cold, bleak snows of my northern home.

But the beauty saddens me—why, I cannot explain!

As for the Laird (I still call him that), he has taken quite kindly to foreign travel and foreign ways. The little difficulties as to baggage, hotels, and money-exchange are made comprehensible by my thorough acquaintance with French, and many Continental journeys, and my husband is perfectly content to pay so long as I can explain the why and wherefore of payment required.

At the present moment he is at the Casino, studying the mysteries of *roulette*, and determining whether it is quite a proper place to take me to this evening, as I have requested.

We have stayed a week at Nice, and now are paying wicked little Monte Carlo a visit. I did not care to go out, and am lazily sitting here at the open window, contemplating the beauty of the scene, and, as I confessed before, making fresh entries in my long neglected journal. What shall I confess to its pages, as to happiness or unhappiness, sorrow or content? They are all blended in my memory as I look back on my few weeks of wedded life. Donald is very, very good to me, very kind, very thoughtful, but there is no use disguising the truth—we are utterly, utterly unsuited to one another. He has not a particle of poetry or romance in his whole nature. He cannot understand why I should rhapsodize over a scene, or cry and laugh at a theatre, if moved to do so by some subtle and perfect piece of acting, or tremble and grow pale at some strain of grand church music, that seems to lift my soul heavenwards independent of ceremonies or, ritual.

No, feelings and emotions such as these seem a riddle unto him, and he looks at me wonderingly, as if I were some strange specimen of humanity such as had never come under his ken before.

I suppose if it were not for the constant travelling, and the novelty and excitement of sight-seeing, and the—to me—never failing interest of hotel life, we should have been heartily sick of each other's society by this time. You see, I am honest to you, my diary, and dare to confess the truth.

But even with sight-seeing, and driving, and railway journeys, and the amusement to be derived from watching one's fellow mortals at hotels, and observing insular prejudices and airs and graces—displayed to the obsequious and not too honest foreigner, who pockets insults and guineas with equal magnanimity— even with all this, I cannot but agree that honeymoons are a mistake.

Perhaps if one were very much in love—— Heigh ho! What is the use of talking nonsense? There is a young couple there in the gardens below, pacing up and down among the palms, and tropical plants and stranger exotics, whom we have come across from time to time. They are honeymooning also, but are in a state of idiotic, engrossed infatuation that is distressing to a well-regulated mind.

I have watched them occasionally with a sort of wondering interest. They never seem to weary of one another, never care apparently for other company. Even at *table-d'hôte*, I have seen her hand slip into his, a chance look of love unutterable flash from their meeting eyes, or caught some tender phrase whispered under cover of the general conversation.

Sometimes I have felt envious of her. She seems so perfectly, entrancedly happy, and he

—he is young, handsome, debonnair, an ideal
bridegroom, and apparently an amusing companion, to judge from the ripples of laughter
I hear, and the perpetual jokes they have in
common.

The Laird seldom laughs, and if I ever venture upon a mild jest or draw his attention to
anything that strikes me as ridiculous, he seems
to weigh the matter long and seriously in his
mind before relaxing even into a smile at it.
This is not encouraging, so I have devoted
myself to drawing *him* out on the subject of
his native land, and find he can get almost
eloquent on that subject—but alas, on that
only.

I suppose the sentiment of clanship is very
strong among Scotch folk—Highlanders especially, and it exists up to the present time,
despite the disbanding of clans after Colloden,
a history that has been poured into my somewhat inattentive ears very frequently.

The Laird is not one of the roving class of
landlords. He and his fathers before him
have rarely left their native moors, even for

other places and towns in their own country. As I have already said, this is Donald's first experience of foreign lands, and perhaps that accounts for his reticence and want of enthusiasm. A deprecatory shake of the head, a sort of " Well, it's no that bad," is about all I can win from him in the way of praise or admiration.

It is somewhat disheartening, I confess. I have never seen him excited or amused. To everything and everybody he displays that unruffled calm, that watchful observance, that unfailing good temper, which is at once so characteristic and so trying in his people.

Nothing disturbs his equanimity, but nothing seems deserving of praise. Even as to climate, when I venture to remark on the delight of sunshine, blue sky, settled weather, he is up in arms to defend his mists, and rains, and bleak cold days of wind and storm. " Three hours of sunshine in the Highlands is worth three weeks of this calm, monotonous glare," he would say, " there is no light and shade, no sudden change of colour,

no contrast of gloom and glory like our skies
and mountains there." And I can but shrug
my shoulders and try to "command my
soul in patience," and wonder why people are
so obstinate in their prejudices.

"Wait till I show you a Highland sunset,"
he would say. Nor can I ever get him to
allow that anything in the way of scenery we
have yet seen is worthy of comparison with the
lochs and hills of his native land—or that
these calm seas deserve to be mentioned in
the same breath with the long rolling surges
that thunder along the Cromarty shores, or
sweep up in stormy waves to Nairn, and
Findhorn, and Burghead?

When a person—especially a Scotch person
—is obstinately prejudiced in favour of their
own particular land, it is hopeless to try and
make them change their opinion. I gave in,
at first protestingly—then resignedly, as be-
hoved a wedded wife—and I have ceased now
to try and rouse any enthusiasm in the heart
of my lord and master on any subject whatever.

Perhaps these facts account for my sudden fit of confidence to my journal.

The sense of utter unsuitability to each other oppresses me more and more. It is not only the gulf of years that lies between us, but the impossibility to think—talk—feel —alike on any given subject.

I feel that I am fast lapsing into depression and unsociability — withdrawing more and more into myself, and every day I assure that self that honeymoons are a great and grievous mistake, and wonder whether after all it would not have been better to remain in the land that has the honour of owning Corrie-moor as one of its possessions.

At least I could have curtailed the length of that period of boredom, or could have had Bella to stay with me, according to promise.

Now I have absolutely no one to speak to, or confide in. How can I expect staid and matter-of-fact Donald to understand the vague whims and fancies, the caprices and exactions, the moods and vagaries, of young womanhood ?

They are all new and strange to him, and he has no key to unlock their mysteries. He constantly dilates on the perfections of his mother, who seems, from his description, to possess every feminine virtue under the sun; but he appears to know very little about women, and has evidently taken her as a model for the rest of her sex.

If they are not like her—they ought to be.

I know I am very, very different. I begin to think he is also on the way to find that out, and that soon—very soon—he will be telling himself that he has made a mistake, and the knowledge of that mistake will shadow all the future of his honest, useful, blameless life.

" Well, I suppose we are not the only people who have done that," I say to myself, somewhat bitterly, as I turn away from the sight of that pair of wedded lovers in the gardens below.

But the reflection is none the more consolatory because of its truth.

With it, however, I close this page of my

journal, and proceed to look out a suitable gown for *table-d'hôte* at seven o'clock.

*   *   *   *   *

It was a strange sight that met my eyes last night when the Laird and I left the brilliant rooms of the Grand Hotel de Paris, and walked across the lovely gardens to the Casino.

With the blundering obstinacy of manhood he had, as I said before, gone over to the rooms in the afternoon to decide whether I might with safety be brought thither *in the evening*.

The difference in the scene must have been startling, or so I imagined from his look of amazement and from my own later experience. The *Salle de Jeu* at 4 p.m. and at 9 p.m. is a very different place. And what a contrast between the scene without, lit by the imperial splendour of moon and stars, and the garish brilliance of the rooms with their gaudy decorations and gilding—their moving, restless crowds—the incessant hum of voices in all languages—the chink of gold and silver—the monotonous cry of the croupiers — the idle, foolish laughter of painted women in airy toilettes and marvellous diamonds, as they pass to and fro with their no less foolish admirers.

A concert was going on in the room set apart for that purpose, but the audience was very scanty. The attractions of the tables certainly outweighed those of the diviner art.

I looked with keen interest at the scene. For me it had all the charm of novelty—all the wonder of the unknown. How absorbed some of the faces—how reckless and anxious others. What histories must have lain hidden under the paint and powder—the beauty and the vileness—the despair and effrontery—the nobility and baseness—that world of physiognomy presented!

"I want to watch the roulette players," I said to the Laird, as we made our way through the brilliant, restless throng.

He glanced uneasily about him, as if fearful of encountering some compatriot or acquaint-

23*

ance who would be shocked and amazed at such a proceeding.

"Indeed I'm thinking it's not a right place for a lady to be in," he said hesitatingly. "It's no ways the same as when I saw it this afternoon. The crowd is just fearful, and certainly most of them look—well, I would not just call it—respectable."

I laughed. I could not help it. He looked so distressed, and so perplexed. To me the types and faces were not so very different from those I had seen in the parks and hotels of Paris and Brussels, or at the races of Longchamps and Baden. But I suppose there was something very shocking and very immoral about both place and people, to my staid and virtuous Donald.

However, I had my way, and we struggled through a mass of skirts and elbows to a vantage point at one of the tables.

There they sat in steady, immovable array —the army of players—white, calm, desperate. All of life and feeling they possessed seemed centred in their eyes. Those strange, glittering, furtive glances fixed on the colour, or the piles of gold and silver, had a horrible fascination for me. I watched them, awed and wondering: the people with systems—the reckless believer in chance—the devotee of a combination of numbers—the cautious calculator of colour.

There they sat, steadfast and engrossed, oblivious to all else but that fatal pastime.

Wizened old women side by side with young girls; men—old, middle-aged, youthful, rich and reckless, or poor and calculating. There seemed contagion in the atmosphere. Suppressed excitement — mirth — triumph — expectation — hope — despair — so ran the gamut of humanity's best and worst emotions.

I stood there, protected by Donald's stalwart form from the pressure of the crowd, and following with vivid interest the chances of the game and the varying luck of the players.

I suppose he did not find so much interest

in it as I did, for he soon began to show signs of impatience.

"Come away, Athole," he entreated at last; "this is no fit place for you. To me it looks just as fearful as hell itself might do."

I turned aside then and followed him through the rooms again, and we left the noise and heat and glare behind us, and went on through the dusky gardens to the beautiful terrace beyond.

The strains of a band floated from the distance. The purple mountains looked down upon us, the moon gleamed like silver in the deep, intense blue above—the sighs of the restless sea came up from the curving shores below. Involuntarily I slipped my hand into Donald's arm, and drew a long deep breath of mingled pain and pleasure.

"Oh, is it not lovely?" I cried, as I stood there on the marble terrace, and drank in with rapture the delights of sense and sight.

"It's no as fair as Loch Fyne," was his reply. "But it's well enough."

CHAPTER VI.

" But sorrow returned with the dawning of morn,
   And the voice in my dreaming ear melted away."

" The day comes to me, but delight brings me nane,
   The night comes to me—but my rest it has gane.
   I wander, my love, like a night-troubled ghaist,
   And I sigh as my heart it wad burst in my breast."

" It's well enough ! "

That is about the height the Laird's admiration ever reaches.

Whether he thinks it a point of honour to uphold the beauties of his native land as superior to all else he may behold, or is really incapable of admiring anything but his Highland lochs and hills, I cannot say, but he certainly will not allow that anything he sees, or over which I rhapsodize, is one whit more beautiful.

It is rather exasperating sometimes. I

hate narrow-minded people, and I have come to the conclusion that Donald is obstinate in his prejudices, and wilfully one-sided in his opinions.

As I am neither familiar enough with him, nor fond enough of him, to argue or coax him into accepting my views, I generally lapse into silence, and leave him to the serene content which his own seem to afford,

*   *   *   *   *

There is no use in making daily entries in my journal. There seems so little to say. We dine, drive, walk, sleep, and, I suppose, mutually bore one another. At least, I can answer for myself.

I am sure I know every landscape of the Corniche Road, every villa between Ville-franche and Eza, every curve of the bay, every aspect of blue sky, blue water, and grey olive woods. I think the warm, sunny air, the breezes laden with scents of acacia and rose boughs, make me languid and melancholy. I begin to wonder how much longer Donald intends to stay here, and to

ask myself whether my own home could be
duller, or more depressing.

For the Laird is strangely unsocial. He
rather avoids the society of his fellow man.
He seems to have a rooted prejudice against
all foreigners, and to consider the men fools,
and the women improper.

Now and then we go to the Concert-room
at the Casino, but once the music is over, I
am hustled away and not allowed a glimpse
at the *Salle de Jeu*, or its glittering crowd of
fashion and notoriety.

We visit Roquebrune and Eza and Men-
tone, spend a day at San Remo, and another
at Antibes, but I am bound to say I have
found them all very much alike, with
the exception of Roquebrune, and that certainly is ancient enough, and picturesque
and dirty enough, to delight any antiquarian
or artist.

The Laird, however, is always grumbling
about "drains," and the general unwhole-
someness of foreign towns, and he sees no
beauty in the dusky roads and the old, dark

houses, and the quaint streets, where the old peasant women sit at their fruit stalls, and the flower-girls offer their roses and violets at every corner, and the little brown children tumble over one another's heads, and watch with big, shy eyes as the strangers stroll along.

So the days glide into weeks, and we have seen everything and done everything, and I at last venture to suggest that we may as well turn our steps homeward.

The Laird agrees readily, and almost rapturously. I suppose he is not sorry his honeymoon is over.

I spend my last evening wandering through the gardens, thinking to myself (I dare not confess it to my lord and master) that never again shall I probably see so lovely a sight as those dusky, starlit glades, with their subtle, exotic scents and softly gleaming lamps, and the dark violet of sea and sky which forms their setting.

Perhaps, in my heart, I am almost sorry to be leaving this place. Before me lies a life wholly new and strange; new scenes, new faces, new duties. A sort of dread seizes me as I think of all it may mean.

Why was I in such a hurry to marry, why did I not remain as I was?

Already I can see that between my husband and myself yawns a great gulf of dissimilarity —that we have no single taste, habit or desire in common.

And I am so young, and I suppose in all likelihood I have many years of life to look forward to, and yet—well I only know it seems to me that the mainspring of such life is for ever broken, that it will drag on—limp on—with a dreary, if safe monotony, until we part company for ever on this material plane.

An epitaph that I had read somewhere will keep running in my head. It seems ridiculous and out of keeping with this beautiful scene, and the gay, chattering idlers scattered about, but all the same I find myself repeating it. It had been inscribed over the grave of one Thomas Price, aged twenty-seven, his wife Mary,

aged twenty-five, and his daughter Mary,
aged two years.

> " Our tyme on earth it were full short,
>   The Will of God was so.
>   Affliction sore did fais on us,
>   So we where forstt to go."

Over and over again the quaint rhymes
ring in my ears, here where the sea is sighing
against the white marbles of the terrace, and
the far-off strains of music float in sudden,
fitful melody from the distant rooms.

" Our time on earth it were full short." I
suppose it was a short life if they were happy,
and yet perhaps father and mother and child
were better off than if one of the family had
lingered behind, to battle with the thorns and
briars of this work-a-day world.

At least they were together so far as we
know. " The will of God was so."

I wonder who put up the inscription ?
Surely not Thomas or Mary, for they could
not have known they were to follow each
other so quickly, and that the child would
hasten after them to the " Unknown Land,"
with such willing feet.

Then I thought of the beautiful cemetery with its Gaelic name and its quaint situation, and of my false lover's wooing there, and the joy that had been so brief.

I think to-night I wish myself at rest under the shade of the rowans and beech trees, to-night, when all the beauty and brightness of the life around me seems covered with the funeral pall of my own sad thoughts and sorrowful forebodings.

Sighing, I turn away, and retrace my steps to the hotel. I have said my farewells to garden and terrace, to Monaco, on its dark, isolated rock, and Condamine, with its pretty harbour, and the far, wide stretch of lemon and orange and olive woods.

"I suppose I shall never come here again," I say to myself, and perhaps the home of the dead and gone Grimaldi gains a new and regretful interest to me from the hour I leave it.

For in due course of time we do leave it, and set our faces homewards and Scotland-wards, and so for many days of wearisome

travel, and depressing weather, and general
fatigue and discomfort, I do not open my
journal, or commit to its silent pages any
information respecting my life, or thoughts,
or surroundings.

In the North again.

How cold, and bleak and dreary it looked
to me after the blue skies and sunshine and
green woods I had left. How I shivered in
my warm furs as I sat in the railway carriage
and looked out at the grey, bleak chain of
the Grampians, and saw the whirling snow
drifting past the windows, and the grey
clouds piled in heavy masses in the grey sky
overhead.

The Laird was stretched full length on the
seat opposite, wrapped in a thick rug and
smoking a huge pipe. He looked comfortable
and serene, facts probably due to the sensation that his foot was once more on his
" native heath."   I had faintly hinted that we
might break our journey at Inverness. I so
longed to see Grannie's sweet, old face, and

hear Bella's cheery voice, but Donald did not respond to the suggestion.

"It is quite time," he said, "that you make my mother's acquaintance, and it will not look just respectful, under the circumstances, that we tarry here with other folk, instead of going to Corriemoor direct."

I therefore said no more, and put the best face I could on the discomforts and fatigues I had to endure.

The train rocked and shook along the rough uneven line, until every bone in my body ached, and my brain felt absolutely stunned.

To read was impossible, and I never could keep up a long conversation with the Laird under the most favourable circumstances. To talk through the din and rattle, and jolting of that fearful Highland railway, was therefore a matter of more than ordinary difficulty. I could only sit there in dumb discomfort, and watch the snow falling over the dismal landscape, and wish in a weak and vain manner that I had stayed in the Riviera for another month.

But the longest day comes to an end, and
so does the longest journey, and at length the
welcome mandate went forth to leave the
train, as we were at the station nearest our
destination. Then followed a long, cold drive
in an open dog-cart, and at last, in the dusk
and gloom of the dying day, I caught sight of
my new home.

Miles and miles of moorland stretched
around, white with the snowfall. The air
was raw and bleak. The gaunt trees looked
doubly gaunt, with their bare branches
stretched skywards, and laden with snow. I
was thankful to take my frozen limbs and
chilled small person into an atmosphere of
warmth and light once more. The hall was
illumined by a blazing fire and the light of
many candles. On the walls were deer
antlers, and other trophies of the chase, and
skins and rugs covered the oaken floor. I
caught sight of pictures of the Laird's family
and clan, evidently dating generations back,
in kilt and armour, and other strange garbs,
and all looking more or less stern and forbid-

ding in their dark frames. My mother-in-law
was standing beside the great open fire-place,
awaiting us. A solemn, stately old dame, in
rich and rustling black satin and antique
lace. Her white hair was plainly braided on
either side her brow; her face was wonder-
fully fresh coloured and unwrinkled considering her age; the blue eyes were keen and
somewhat stern, but their expression softened
as they rested on the tired and drooping
figure which the Laird led up to her for
welcome. "My wife, mother," he said
simply, and something in the pride and
tenderness of his tone touched me deeply.
I felt the tears rush to my eyes, and I
trembled from head to foot.

The stately old lady took me in her arms,
and kissed me warmly. "Welcome, my
daughter," she said, in that sweet, low,
drawling voice which is so peculiarly Scotch,
and as characteristic—to my thinking—
as the accent itself. "I'm sure you're
weary after so long a journey. I'll just take
ye to your ain room, and ye shall have a

sleep and rest before dinner. We can bide an hour for that, eh, Donald?"

"Certainly," said her son heartily. "Only I'll just have a dram to keep out the cold, while you take Athole upstairs. Could you not give her some hot tea for herself, mother? She's almost frozen, poor bairn."

"It is all ready for her," said the old lady, and I was whisked off and taken into a large, comfortably-furnished bedroom, where a big fire blazed cheerily, before which a great old-fashioned couch was drawn up.

My mother-in-law herself assisted me to remove my hat and wraps, and a neat Scotch maid unpacked my trunk, and gave me one of my dressing-gowns, and I then was ordered to lie down on the big couch, and covered up with an eider-down quilt, and tea was brought in by the maid, Flora, and a delicious sense of rest and comfort and warmth stole over my tired frame.

I grew very drowsy, and the old lady noticed it, and left me to sleep till dinner-time.

The Laird came to waken me, but I was so spent and exhausted that he refused to let me come downstairs, so I had dinner sent to me there, and after dinner retreated to bed and slept the deep, dreamless sleep of sheer bodily fatigue, until the maid knocked at my door next morning.

*   *   *   *   *

I have made a tour of the house, and been introduced to the old servants, and now am sitting in my own room posting up my journal.

The snow is still falling heavily. The lookout from the windows is desolate in the extreme. But I feel rested and soothed and fairly content. Everyone has been very kind to me. The Laird, too, is far more genial and cheery in his own home than ever I have known him out of it.

I like this quaint old house, with its rambling passages and dark old-fashioned rooms and great fire places. The old lady is never weary of relating anecdotes and histories of their people, of whose deeds of

24*

valour and virtue there seems to be an endless catalogue.

The Laird's own room—study, as they call it—is mainly conspicuous for an absence of everything conducive to, or associated with, that word. It is hung round with trophies of the chase—guns, fishing-rods, golf-sticks, curling-stones, stuffed birds in cases, and great eagles and falcons perched on stands and brackets. I have never seen such a room, and he is very proud indeed of it.

My own bedroom is very large, with a deep bay-window at one end, commanding a view of moor and hill and deer-forest. Part of it is furnished like a sitting-room, with writing-table, chairs, couch, work-stand, and very comfortable and pleasant it looks in the ruddy warmth of the fire-light, despite the grey sky and heavy snow-clouds without.

On the whole I feel very well content, though I doubt but the life here will be monotonous enough.

My mother-in-law has somewhat formally proffered me the duties of housekeeping should I wish to undertake them, but I plead inexperience and ignorance, and beg her to continue as she has always done. I am quite content to be second in the household. I can see the old lady is pleased at this, and so no doubt are the servants.

So begins my married life in my Scotch home. Romance is a folded leaf in a book that must never again be opened.

I look on these pages, having made up my mind to lock them away and forget — if possible—the dreams and follies and regrets that they record.

One sigh for the youth that was so brief, the love that was so false, the hopes that were so futile.

One sigh—Oh, Douglas, Douglas! . . .

A tear follows the sigh—it rests on his name—the name that has cost me so many tears.

Will this be the last I shall shed for him?

God grant it. Good-bye, Douglas. . . . Good-bye, Youth. Good-bye, Love.

BOOK III.

CHAPTER I.

"Then gently scan your brother man,
Still gentler—sister woman ;
Though they may gang a keenin' wrang
To step aside is human.

    *   *   *   *   *

" What's done we partly may compute,
But know not what's resisted."

YOUTH is headstrong and impetuous. That is no new thing to say ; we have all heard it often enough.

I suppose it was only natural that I, Douglas Hay, scapegrace and ne'er-do-weel as I had always been called, should have consumed most of my hot-headed youthful days in longings to be free and untrammelled, to escape the burden of conventionality, and the boredom of narrow-mindedness, and the mixture of cant and shrewdness, psalm-singing, kirk-going, and money-getting, which to my mind represented my nation, or such of it as had come under my ken.

My mother I had never known. My father was a tyrant in disposition and a miser in habits—my home a dreary and unhappy one, against which I had instinctively rebelled, and which, to my youthful mind, had repre-sented only a place of punishment, fault-finding and hardships.

I must frankly confess I never willingly spent an hour there that I could possibly spend anywhere else, and that my father was never sorry to see my back turned on his demesnes.

If floggings, and semi-starvation, and sarcasm are good food for bringing up a child, then assuredly I should have been a model of excellence, but as the character I bore in my native place was that of a " born reprobate," I can only suppose the treatment signally failed in what it was intended to do for me. Pious elders of the Kirk shook their heads as they passed me by. Worthy mothers of families tried the effects of " a word in season," but their idea of " season " invariably clashed with mine, and the seed never sprang up, or took any root worth speaking of.

I went to school, and having a fair amount of ability, I managed to acquire as much knowledge as the generality of boys ever do. The masters always said I might have done better, but, as a rule, they are a race niggardly of praise and impossible to please. I made little attempt to win either praise or satisfaction from them, and they reported me to my father according to their judgment and opinion.

Needless to say it differed somewhat from my own.

When school-days were over, the question of my future course was mooted, and here again I and the author of my being were very widely opposed in our views. I wished to be a soldier. He would not hear of it, but was bent upon my entering the church. This I resolutely refused to do, and while the battle waged I led a very idle and reprehensible life.

I was fond of gaiety and amusement. I desired above all things experience, and I set to work to gain it in whatever way seemed to me good. Women petted me and were fond of me. I had the talent or facility which makes a young man popular, that is to say I was a fair musician, a good dancer, an excellent shot, and possessed of indefatigable energies and spirits.

The women took me up and the men abused me, between them they afforded me plenty of amusement and occupation. I was as seldom at home as I could help, and the gulf between my father and myself grew wider and wider as time went on, and I was too old to be tyrannized over, and too independent to be bullied.

An old aunt, whom I had never seen, died suddenly and left me about fifty pounds a year. It was not much, but it made me independent of my father, and though the miser's side of his nature rejoiced at the saving of expense, the tyrannical was displeased at the comparative freedom and independence I could now enjoy.

I went to Edinburgh and to Glasgow, delighted with the new sense of liberty. I made plenty of friends and acquaintances, some perhaps less safe than others, but what cares youth for danger, or risk, or reputability?

I went back to my native town after one of these visits to the capital, and there for the first time I met the Fate that sooner or later overtakes all manhood. I did not at first understand what such a meeting might mean for me. I did not think it was in me to care seriously or deeply for any feminine thing. For their own sakes I am sorry to say they had led me to consider them in a very light and depreciative manner. But somehow this small slip of girlhood, with her wistful little face and big, dark, solemn eyes, touched some chord in my nature as yet unawakened or recognised even by myself.

She was so innocent, so young, there was
something about her so altogether fragile and
pathetic, that she seemed to attract love and
tenderness as naturally as a child. How easy
it was to win her interest, to make that
interest ripen into something warmer, deeper,
more passionate. The baseness of rivalry was
not wanting as an incentive, had I needed
such. I could see her cousin Kenneth cared
for her from the first, but he was a cold and
cautious wooer, and it needed little effort on
my part to push him out of the field. A more
formidable rival, however, arose in the shape
of the Laird of Corriemoor, one of the richest
and best-known of Highland land-owners, and
who had fallen, I plainly saw, an easy victim
to the little winsome lass who was everyone's
pet and favourite.

Even as I write these words the sense of my
own baseness and ingratitude underlies them
each and all.

She loved me so truly and so deeply, and
I—well, God knows, I loved her too, but
that did not prevent my behaving as only

a scoundrel and a coward would have behaved.

Often I ask myself, why? Even now it is somewhat of a mystery to me. Now, when the wide seas roll between us, and she and I may in all probability touch hands in love, or friendship, never—never more!

In these long, lonely nights, pacing to and fro the deck of the ship that bears me further and further away, how often I have thought of her, with what a mingling of regret, and sorrow and desire. And yet what could have come of our love but misfortune and un-happiness? Everyone opposed it, and I could not blame them for doing so.

I had sown my reputation years before, by many an ill deed, and careless word, and idle habit. What other harvest could I expect to reap than the one I had gathered in?

Some sudden fit of remorse and disgust with myself, and the influence brought to bear on me by another woman, resulted in an abrupt break between Athole Lindsay and myself.

I knew that woman was unworthy to be

named in the same breath with the girl I loved.
She was a syren made to snare men's fancies
and appeal to their worst instincts. Their
conquest had long been to her an easy matter.
I read her very clearly from the first, and
the reading amused me, as did the pretty,
subtle love-making, so thinly disguised under
the friendly interest and attention she bestowed
on me.

Heaven knows I don't say this out of vanity.
I seemed but a boy in years to Mrs. Dunleith,
and she affected to treat me as such. What
broke down her guard, and enlightened me as
to her feelings, was her jealousy of Athole
Lindsay. One night that jealousy burst forth
as a slumbering fire long hidden may do, and
then I found myself caught in that whirlwind
of passion, reproach, anger, and desire, which
some women call love.

The scene was terrible, the more so because
unexpected, and by me certainly undeserved.
I soothed her as best I could, and, in somewhat cowardly fashion perhaps, made light of
her suspicions with regard to Athole. I

declared there was no engagement between us, and the announcement seemed to content her. Then, to cut the Gordian knot of my difficulties, and seeing plainly that the Laird of Corriemoor was very much in earnest in his attentions, I took myself off suddenly and without notice or farewell to either Mrs. Dunleith, or Athole.

I went to Edinburgh, and sulked there in smouldering misery, that longed to vent itself on someone, and yet was perfectly aware of its own inability to do so. It had been selfish and self-sought, and I could see no way out of it.

A brave and more unselfish nature would never have set itself to win a young girl's heart and love for no better purpose than its own gratification.

I see that all so plainly now, but I did not see it then, or was it that I needed the sharp touch of sorrow's lash to teach me my lesson?

In a state of wrath, disgust and dissatisfaction, I lingered for a while in Edinburgh, and then wrote to Athole to free her from the obligation I felt I had in some way forced upon her.

I think now my letter must have seemed cruel to her, though I meant it for the best. In the mood I was in at that time, I was not capable of calm or temperate judgment. I set her free, and perhaps only in those long weeks of silence that followed on her part, did I begin to feel how much I really cared for her. Then Mrs. Dunleith appeared on the scene again. But she chose a new *rôle* now.

The syren was laid aside, and the friend took her place. Tender sympathy, warm interest, frank and cordial companionship —these were all at my service, veiled now and then by some word or tone or look which recalled, without alarming, the old memories and the old days.

I should have been more than mortal man to resist the gradual influence that was brought to bear upon my life at that time, when I was most reckless and most unhappy.

I wondered why a woman so beautiful, and so formed to attract men, as Dora Dunleith, should care to waste her thoughts and attentions on me. I made but poor return Heaven knows.

Yet she never seemed to resent my *brusquerie*, or my coldness. Perhaps, now that she knew her rival was out of the field, she felt she could wait with patience.

An older man might have yielded to the transient and subtle delights such intercourse and society afforded, if only to lull conscience and win forgetfulness. But I only felt irritated and ashamed at my own weakness.

In my love for Athole, there had been purity and poesy. A sentiment of the soul, a vague delight that made even self-torment a pleasure. It had been something to walk for miles, only to see the light in her window, or catch a glimpse of her sweet face from afar, or even the chance of meeting her in the High Street with her inseparable companion, Bella Cameron. These are the foolish trivialities in which youth delights.

* * * * *

How my head aches, to-night! How weary

and disheartened I feel. I have been sitting in moody reflection over these pages, writing, and reading, and thinking, and in my heart cursing my folly, and wondering what possessed me to accept Dora Dunleith's proposition to go to Canada to seek my fortune.

What does fortune matter to me? For whose sake should I do battle with the world? At whose hand seek the guerdon of victory, or the soft sympathy that compassionates failure? There is no doubt that some natures need the ballast of another to steady and control them. Disappointment has a deteriorating effect. They plunge into dissipation as a distraction. Billiards, late hours, smokes and drinks, and play, have the advantage of bringing temporary excitement and forgetfulness. Women—more wise, and hampered by worldly prejudices and shut in by that thick set hedge of conventionality, which the innate weakness of the feminine heart knows as a safe-guard, even if an irksome one—they, as I say, more wisely take to religion, or

Sunday school teaching, and are martyrs, in a quiet, unimpassioned way of their own.

Perhaps they are less actively unhappy than we are, but the grey hues of hidden sorrow settle none the less surely over their lives.

*   *   *   *   *

How the wind howls to-night. Surely a storm is brewing. I can write no more. I will go up on deck, and see how the weather looks.

After all, it is rather a womanish piece of weakness to commit the incidents of one's life to paper.

But time hangs heavy on my hands now, and I have not yet fraternized much with my fellow-passengers.

That is my excuse, though why I offer it to the paper I am rapidly spoiling, I am at a loss to say.

CHAPTER II.

" Man is his own star, and the soul that can
   Render an honest and a perfect man
   Commands all light, all influence, all fate ;
   Nothing to him falls early, or too late ;
   Our acts our angels are, or good or ill,
   Our fatal shadows, that walk by us still."

THE storm was raging frightfully when I stepped on deck. I could scarcely keep my footing in the teeth of the furious gale.

As I clung to one of the shrouds, I saw a figure beside me, occupied in the same endeavour to preserve his equilibrium.

It was that of a man, one of my fellow-passengers, whom I had noticed several times already. The singularity of his face and features, or rather the expression that stamped them, were sufficient to attract observation.

Young enough in years, to all appearances yet the face itself was one strangely impassive,

25*

the eyes cold and hard, the mouth drawn into
firm lines, its expression bitter and cynical in
a marked degree.

The brow was lofty and intellectual, the
brow of a student and a thinker, and at rare
moments the eyes lost their hardness and
indifference, and scintillated with excitement
or interest. Now, as I glanced up at him,
and saw them in the fitful moonlight that
struggled through rifts of cloud, they were
absolutely blazing with delight and excitement.

"It is magnificent, is it not?" he said to
me, tossing back the dark waves of hair from
his uncovered head, and looking like some
spirit of the storm in his towering height, and
with that strange, pale face, and those flashing
eyes piercing the gloom and disdaining the
warfare of the elements. "How feeble and
weak after all, is the skill of man against the
forces of nature. Who shall bridle the wind,
and arrest the thunder-cloud, or steer the
lightning flash on its wild flight? Look
yonder at that seething mass. How the

white horses toss their manes and gallop over
the wild sea to-night! Ah, is it not grand,
glorious, superb? What a pity that at such
a time one cannot resolve oneself into something less material than flesh and blood, and
enjoy it as the spirit of the tempest itself
might do!"

I looked at him in some surprise. The
words were strange, but no less strange was
his look and aspect.

"It certainly is a grand sight," I agreed.
"But scarcely enjoyable under present circumstances."

"There I differ from you," he said, the
clear, resonant tones of his voice sounding
distinct even amidst the noise and fury of the
blast. "At all times, and under all aspects,
nature is to me enjoyable. She and I have
been close friends all the years of my life."

"You have travelled greatly?" I suggested,
with another glance at the strange face, un-
youthful even in its youth, yet with something grand and majestic now in its defiant,
fearless pose, and flashing glances.

"Not half as much as I could desire," he said. "That is where life hits one so hard. In youth we are bond-slaves to the possible enjoyments of a future, setting all our energies to work in order to achieve a goal that promises all we deem best. Does age ever fulfil these promises? I doubt it. The years pass, and Time lays a heavy hand upon our spirits and desires, our very nature alters, and the fruition we once upheld as bliss to our fond imaginings, becomes but Dead Sea fruit in our mouths at last."

"You talk very bitterly," I said.

A temporary lull had taken place. The wind blew with less fury, the driving clouds parted here and there to show some gleam of star or moon in the blue depths of unveiled sky. We were still standing side by side, still clinging to the stout cordage as support. The ship sped on over the foaming waters with scarce a yard of canvas spread from her bending masts.

My companion looked down at me for the first time.

"So you think I speak bitterly," he said. "If so, life has been my teacher. I can but speak of it as I have found it and seen it. Who ends it as he intended? Who finds it as he imagined it? Who looks out from any standpoint in the moral, social, or physical scale, and can truthfully assert that it is anything but vexation and vanity? The wisest man the world has ever known said that, and his judgment will pass unchallenged for all time. Here and there comes a little sunshine, a little pleasure, a little hope—but set against them the toil and weariness, the sorrow and heartaches, the misery and deception and disappointment, that we raise and cause as we journey along that road from youth to age, and dare then to say that the little good is not outweighed a thousand-fold by the many evils—that the sips of pleasure are not as a drop in the ocean to the seas of grief. But see, the storm rises again! We shall have a rough night of it."

"You seem rather to enjoy the prospect," I said, glancing somewhat enviously at the tall figure and the fearless, defiant pose of the uncovered head, where the wind played at will amongst the dark, thick locks.

"Yes," he said quietly, "I am altogether without fear, and yet I and danger have claimed pretty close acquaintance with each other in my time. I have been twice ship-wrecked, but it has not destroyed my love of the sea—nothing could do that."

I felt that I could not agree with him. Indeed, I was already cold and chilled, and wet with spray and rain, and felt more dis-posed to seek my cabin than to watch the storm renew its attentions.

I therefore bade my new acquaintance good-night, and went below, though I must confess sleep was utterly impossible.

Wide awake I lay in my narrow berth, listening to the howling wind and the dashing waves, and the tramp of the sailors' feet on the deck above. How little there seemed between life and death on that wild ocean, in that wild night—only a few planks, the weak armament of man against the warfare of the furious elements. I thought of my strange companion, and wondered if he still was on deck, breasting the storm with that undaunted mien. I almost envied him his supreme enjoyment. I had certainly experienced more fear than pleasure at the sight of the raging sea and the noise of the creaking timbers.

*   *   *   *   *

In the midst of my wakeful meditations I was roused by a fearful crash. I sprang up, and, half dressed as I was, hurried on deck. One of the masts had broken, and lay half on, half over, the deck, a mass of straining cordage and flapping canvas. The sailors were hewing vigorously at it — foremost among them towered the tall figure of my new acquaintance. His face was still calm and unmoved—his coolness and nerve seemed to encourage the men, and they laboured with a will at their task, until the ship was free of the strain and once more rode merrily over the wild waste of waters.

Five minutes later, however, a fresh alarm

arose.   We had sprung a leak, and the order
was given to man the pumps.

For hours and hours—long after the grey
dawn had broken—that weary labour went
on.   One and all—passengers and crew alike
—we gave our willing aid, and again I
noticed foremost to help and encourage,
and with the strength and zest of two
ordinary men, was that strange being who
had seemed to me like the spirit of the
storm itself.

As time went on the reports grew more
and more disheartening—the leak was gaining
on us, and the sea was still terribly heavy.
The men's faces began to look gloomy, and
their energies showed signs of the prolonged
strain.   The wind had abated somewhat, but
the ship pitched and rolled in most distressing fashion in the great trough of heaving
waters.

We had been driven miles out of our course
and the captain could only give a guess as to
our whereabouts.   Till near mid-day they
laboured on at a task which grew hourly

more hopeless. That the ship must be abandoned seemed a growing conviction in the minds of the men, but I must confess it was with no pleasant feeling that I heard the order given to lower the boats. It seemed to me impossible that any boat could live in such a sea, and the gloomy faces around seemed to echo my conviction.

However, the time soon came when we were left with no other alternative. The leak was gaining on us so rapidly that the pumps were abandoned. Provisions and water were handed into the boats, the passengers collected a few clothes and valuables and waited resignedly for the order to leave the vessel.

The captain, I, and the strange passenger—whose name, I had learnt by this time, was Huel Penryth — were the last to quit the doomed vessel.

We cast off and lay at a little distance, watching her as she rolled in that helpless, water-logged manner from side to side, each moment seeming as if it must be her last.

It was a melancholy spectacle, and one destined to live long in my memory. Suddenly she lifted her stern out of the boiling trough, and we saw her bows plunge forward—for a brief space she seemed almost standing upright, and I could not resist a shudder of horror as I looked. A moment and the great waves rolled upwards like living things, ready to seize upon their promised prey; then came the rending sound of breaking spars and crashing timber, and she plunged downwards into the fathomless depths, and the boiling foam rushed, seething and hissing, over the place that should know her no more.

*   *   *   *   *

I looked around after one involuntary exclamation which had escaped us.

A grey sky, half obscured by mist — a waste of heaving water, on which our boat tossed like a cork. That was all I saw— that and the pale, grave faces of my fellow-sufferers.

"May God have mercy on us!" 1 cried

below my breath; but the hopelessness and the peril of our situation seemed to mock that faint petition as we drifted on through the grey mists and the tossing clouds of foam.

CHAPTER III.

A NEW FRIEND.

" Seldom he smiles—
     Or smiles in such a sort
   As if he mock'd himself—and scorn'd his spirit
     That could be moved to smile at anything."
          *   *   *   *
        " .   .   .   .   .   The state of man,
     Like to a little kingdom, suffers then
     The nature of an insurrection."

I WONDER if at any period of my life I shall
be able to look back upon that awful time
without a shudder of horror. I had read of
shipwrecks, and peril, and adventures, and
enjoyed the excitement of so doing. Reality
was a very different thing.

We suffered cold, hunger, thirst — the
hourly dread of death, as our frail boat
tossed helplessly amidst the heavy seas that
threatened to overwhelm it—and days and
nights passed on, and our scanty stock of

provisions was fast drawing to an end, when rescue came.

We were then picked up by a vessel bound for New Guinea, and there I landed—penniless and friendless—to begin life again as best I could. My papers and letters of introduction to the people in Canada were all lost. I knew that I could write to Mrs. Dunleith and tell her of my misfortunes, but I felt no inclination to do so. I did not wish to ask or receive a favour at her hands.

Through the kindness of the Captain whose ship had rescued us, I and my fellows in misfortune were lodged with some people in the town, but, kind and hospitable as they were, I knew that the accommodation could only be temporary.

I took counsel with Huel Penryth, between whom and myself a sort of friendship had sprung up. I cannot honestly say that in my heart I liked him, there was something so hard and cynical about the man, and yet I knew he was brave and enduring, and kind-hearted. Our joint misfortunes and sufferings had proved that. He seemed to like me, and, thrown together as we were, it was only natural that I should explain my situation to him.

He listened in silence, his strange cold eyes fixed on my face, as if reading there what my lips might not choose to reveal.

"Your friend is a woman?" he said quietly, when I had finished.

I coloured slightly, and nodded.

"Perhaps you are wise in not renewing your obligations," he went on. "The question is, do you wish her to know that you have been saved from shipwreck, or remain under the impression that you were drowned?"

"It matters very little to me what she or anyone else believes," I said bitterly. "My life or death concerns no one."

"In that case," he said, "throw in your fortune with me. You are young, you have no ties, you should be adventurous. As for me, the world is all the same, and one country as good as another. With hands to work, and brains to guide, a man should

never be helpless. Gold, glory, pleasure, they
are prizes to be won on the field of enter-
prise. Of the first I have enough and to
spare for both of us. You shall accept as a
loan, what I do not even need, or value.
Let us go to the New World. There one's
energies are not cramped, one's actions para-
lyzed by an effete civilization, or the tyranny
of social distinctions. There man is man, his
own value what he chooses to make it—the
current of thought a pure and undisturbed
stream, not a turbulent river, swollen by the
affluents of chicanery, rivalry, finance, and
self-aggrandisement. Say—will you throw in
your lot with mine? I have long desired a
companion, young, free, enterprising. You
possess those attributes. On my side, I offer
you the half of a fortune I do not need, the
results of an experience you yourself lack,
and a companionship and fidelity that needs
no bond but its own promise."

He held out his hand. His strange eyes
had a warm and kindly light, his face had
lost much of its hard and bitter cynicism.

I took the proffered hand. I was, indeed, deeply moved by his words and his evident sincerity.

"So be it," I said heartily. "For the fortune you offer I accept just as much as bare necessity demands, until I can repay the loan. For the rest——"

"Let the future prove its worth," he said gravely. "I ask no more. It is settled."

*   *   *   *   *

I cannot set down in detail the events of the year that followed. It was adventurous, wild, hazardous, exhilarating beyond that given to most men of this nineteenth century to experience. My strange friend was one of the most gifted and intelligent beings it has ever been my lot to know. Brilliant, daring, with physical strength that seemed to defy hardship, and a sublime audacity that was absolutely devoid of fear — never was man more fitted for the life of peril and excitement which was ours. My roving tastes were gratified to their fullest extent, and I learnt to dispense with many of the false and foolish habits and desires which civilization has named " necessities." I learnt to know how few and small are really those so - called necessities. How bountiful is Nature to the seeker and student of her lore, and how poor our wisdom often looks beside her mysteries, stored up and held close to her silent breast from the world's infancy ; in what blindfold, blundering fashion we most of us go through life, deaf and heedless to all that does not materially concern our individual interests, and petty ambitions.

I was greatly puzzled by my friend's nationality, and he for long was extremely reticent on the point. He spoke several languages, and all fluently and with ease. He had, from his own account, travelled a great deal, studied deeply, read and thought more than many men double his age, and yet with all that expenditure of thought and study had never adopted any profession, or settled down into any given groove.

I think his intellect was of the militant order, and that he made more foes than

26*

friends by the boldness of his opinions and
the absolute intolerance he had for all deception or pandering to prejudices. He was
enamoured of progress, and the field of
research was to him an inexhaustible delight.

We had a turn at gold-mining in Australia,
for six months, and his knowledge and skill,
added to his great physical strength, resulted
in a venture so successful that I, at least,
could have commanded independence for life.
But the roving fever was in my veins now,
and I felt no inclination to realize my fortune
and settle down into the tame and mediocre
respectability of a citizen's life.

Huel was a born democrat, yet it never
seemed to me he could have sprung from the
people. He had no vicious tastes either, and
possessed a nature too cold and critical to
have ever succumbed to the influence or
caprice of women. Indeed, his indifference
to the sex amused me often, though I knew
it was the outcome of a genuine feeling.

"They are only butterflies in the garden of
life," he said to me when I argued with him

that there might be some good and virtue and
gentleness in the sex he so scathingly con-
temned. "Pretty enough, I grant, in the
sunshine and flowers, but useless when sorrow
—necessity—hardship demand sympathy, or
aid, or intelligence."

I thought then that some deeper motive
than he chose to confess had made him adopt
such opinions. He had suffered, and deeply
too, at the hands of one woman ere he could
thus condemn and despise the whole sex.
But I never attempted to force his confidence.
I knew that if the mood or inclination ever
took him I should hear the story of his life,
and if I was at times curious respecting it, I
knew better than to display the feeling.

I had soon discovered that Huel Penryth
was a materialist—possessing absolutely no
belief in the usually received creeds to which
men pin their faith, and by which they
establish their various forms of worship. The
boldness and frankness, as well as the cold,
cruel truths of his unsparing logic, at first
rather startled me, but he made no attempt

to force his views and opinions on my mind, nor would he ever obtrude them unasked. Face to face with Nature as we were, it was no difficult matter to prove the simple, unerring method of her proceedings in all matters, however small or insignificant.

"It is man who intrudes and upsets, or tries to upset, her work," he said. "Man, who refuses to be content, and sets his pompous pride and vanity against her simple proofs. Miracles! Why should there be miracles? They were never needed save to terrify or coerce the feeble-minded into recognizing a superior power, which their spiritual tyrants declared to be vested in their own persons. There has always been cause and effect, a rational result for any rational need. Why should the whole laws of Nature undergo a change to give birth to one being more than another? The immutable laws of Life and Death stood from the beginning, framing a necessity, and subject to perfectly natural human desires. As Night to Day, so Death to Life comes as its resting-time after its seasons of helplessness, labour, fruition. Here and there a great enthusiast, or a great theory have produced a fierce sensationalism in man's mind, and there has sprung up a so-called Religion, which again has filtered through ambitious or dogmatic or superstitious minds, until its origin has been lost in the pomp and splendour that overlaid it, or the petty warfares that stripped it of original purity or simplicity. Religion may be man's effort to reach a superior Being he recognises ; I cannot see in it the desire of that Being to bring man into touch with, or knowledge of himself."

"It is characteristic of humanity," I ventured to say. "There seems to have been always the recognition of a superior power or Being, and the effort to worship that power in a suitable manner seems to imply that religion is a necessity, though its forms may be mistaken and liable to perverse and erroneous dealings."

"It is characteristic of weakness," he answered. "The desire to lean on another's strength, and be guided by another's authority."

"But," I argued, "without some form of religion, man would not be governable."

He smiled—that cold, cynical smile I knew so well.

"There you hit the secret of priestcraft, the earliest form of government," he said. "To coerce, it was necessary to terrify—to convince, it was necessary to amaze—to attract, it was necessary to charm—so we have Hell for the first purpose, miracles for the second, and ritual for the last."

"But though the Form is of man's creating, there is some deeper root to religious belief than mere speculation. You yourself grant a Creative force, may not that which is so marvellous be called Divine?"

"I certainly grant that force. One finds it in every analysis of Nature. But it is simply a result of the organic forces, which proceed from one another by various modifications."

"Still," I persisted, "something—someone —must have set that force in motion. Trace

it back as far as you may, you still reach that
stumbling block of all theories, ' The First.'
Let it be germ, form, force, there has been
design in it. The fact of man being unable to
comprehend the nature and origin of the
Designer seems a proof that that nature is
above his own—superior to his mental
faculties, and therefore worthy of his
reverence. We are mysteries to ourselves;
we cannot understand that strange duality
which seems compounded of the animal and
the god. We can but say, ' We are.' Our
own wills have nothing to do with our
existence or its termination."

"So, because you cannot understand why
' you are,' you attribute the fact that you
exist to a spiritual Being shrouded in mystery
and labelled, ' Incomprehensible,' rather than
to the natural results of organic life," said
Huel scoffingly. " The world is crowded with
inutility, it holds monsters, abortions, things
noxious and injurious as well as useful. Why
force the responsibility of their existence on a
personal Creator, instead of adopting the

more rational theory which I uphold? The accidental encounter of many forces has given birth to all forms of life, but only those which correspond to the conditions of their surroundings, survive, and transform themselves, and become perfected by various stages of evolution through which they are compelled to pass. If you demand a Creator, you must allow He is a very imperfect one, otherwise, everything would have been what you are pleased to call Him—perfect."

"You yourself said that our minds, being on a lower scale, might find it impossible to comprehend their own origin?"

"True; but if the outcome of perfect reason and perfect power, they could never have been incomplete. I know humanity clings to that idea of a superior power, a personal interest in its faiths and feelings—to me, it is the childish folly of superstition; but I grant you that superstition has a strong hold on man, and has been fostered and upheld through the darkest and cruellest stages of history. If I had found that a Personal Superintendence over man's life averted misfortune, or prevented the ills, and sorrows, and pains, and sufferings, which are as surely his fate as the air he breathes, I might adopt that theory. But as it is, I prefer to believe in the fecundity of matter and the purely natural results of rational natural laws. Let the mind which must bow to a superior will and recognise infallibility in error and cruelty, lay to itself the superstition that pleases it best, and deck its fallacies in any garb or ritual it admires. For my part, I have no faith in theology, nor have I succeeded in discovering any reason for submitting my will and giving up my freedom of thought to the control of any other being, no wiser or more reasonable than myself. Yet that is what Religion would compel me to do; I therefore turn my back on it. My doing so need not distress humanity; if I am wrong, I shall suffer; if they are wrong, they will do likewise. There is the case in a nutshell. Come, don't look at me as if I were a demon, I shall not attempt to overthrow your beliefs, I promise you.   Like to unlike is far better ground for friendship, than perfect accord!"

CHAPTER IV.

IN THE BUSH

" The common growth of mother earth
　Suffices me, her tears, her mirth,
　Her humblest mirth and tears."

*　　*　　*　　*　　*

" The world is too harsh with us, late and soon,
　Getting and spending we lay waste our powers."

THE first burst of the Australian spring was to me a wonder and delight.

The pale tints, the chill air, the variable climate, of my own native land were a good preparation for the splendour of colour, and the wealth of sunshine, and the almost oppressive fragrance of this new world. The air was laden with the scents of acacias and fruit blossoms, and the rich untrained luxuriance of flowers and creepers decked even the wildest spots with beauty.

We were staying, for a time, at one of the big sheep runs on the Emu River. Huel had made the acquaintance of its owner, and accepted the frank offer of his hospitality with equal frankness.

To me, the change was mightily pleasant, for I had had a rough time of it at the gold-fields. Our host was a Scotchman, Robert McKaye by name, who had come out to the colony when quite a young man, and now had amassed a large fortune, and married and settled down there. He had two daughters, Jessie and Janet by name, very bright, pretty girls, and able to ride, shoot, and manage dairy and household in a fashion that would have surprised some of their hot-house nurtured sisterhood in the old country.

I was delighted with them and their life in general. They were frank, clever, companionable, without the slightest affectation of manner, and had managed to educate themselves surprisingly. They even had a piano, and I won their eternal gratitude by tuning and screwing it up into playable condition. In the evenings I would play and sing the old Scotch airs and melodies and dances for Mr. McKaye, and often have I seen the great tears roll down his rugged sunburnt face as the familiar words and airs brought back the memories of his own youth and his unforgotten country.

"Once a Scot, always a Scot," is very true. I think no men are so loyal in their attachment to their native land, so tenacious of upholding their nationality, so proud of their ancestry and descent!

That spring-time in the big house by the beautiful river was, to me, one of those resting places in life which are like a landmark to look back upon in after years. Even Huel grew social and genial amidst those kindly natures, and the freedom and unconventionality of our life with them.

I never heard him scoff at the old Scotchman's habits and opinions, or the tenacity with which he clung to the simple form of his religious faith.

Perhaps the straightforward, honest nature of the man himself, answered better than any argument as to the worth of that faith, and the reality of that religion.

One evening, we were all sitting out in the verandah, the men smoking, the women working, and the conversation turned upon the old country. I had asked Mr. McKaye if he intended ever returning there.

" Well, I'll no say the thought has not been in my mind," he answered, with that due caution of speech so characteristic of his race. " But," he added, with a hurried glance at the two eager faces of the girls, " there's time enough yet."

" Father always says that," pouted pretty Jessie, the youngest of the daughters. " I'm sure he'd be glad to leave here and see Scotland. He's never tired of talking about it and praising it, and yet he won't ever promise to take us there. I'm sure he could well leave this place in the care of the headman, Robertson. He's as careful and conscientious as anyone could be. We might run over to the old country for a year and look up some of our kin. It's hard to know none of them."

" Where would be the advantage ? " asked the old Scotchman gruffly. " Who ever found kinsfolk, or friends either, willing to help one in misfortune, or give one a lift in the world. They're wary enough of approaching you so long as they think you might be asking anything of them. Of course it's another matter when you're well to-to, and independent."

" Have you kept up any correspondence or acquaintance with your folk since you left Scotland ? " asked Huel Penryth carelessly.

"I'm not a good hand at letter-writing," said McKaye. " Once in a twelvemonth or thereabouts I get a letter or write one. My own father and mother are dead long since— some uncles and aunts and cousins in Glasgow are my nearest relatives. They do not trouble their heads about me. I have one friend who writes pretty regularly—we were at school together, but he stuck to the old country, being more favoured of Fortune than I was. He is a landowner and has a fine place of his own in the Highlands. My folk

were only plain Glasgow merchants. Might
you know anything of Scotland?" he asked,
turning suddenly to Huel Penryth.

"No, I have never been there," he said.

"I'm a Cornishman by birth, but I left my
native place too young to remember much
about it."

I glanced with some curiosity at my friend.
It was the first time I had ever heard him
voluntarily state anything about himself.

"Aye, they're a fine race," said McKaye.
"And it's a fine country too, I've heard."

"It is very beautiful," said Huel quietly
and without enthusiasm. "But I've been
a wanderer so long that I've no special
attachment for any one place or part of the
globe. I'm absolutely unpatriotic."

A barking of dogs sounded at this moment,
and then the tramp of horse's hoofs and the
now familiar "coo-ee."

The girls sprang up in wild excitement.

"The waggons," they exclaimed, "and
not before they're wanted. Stores are
running low."

We all rose and went out to where the heavy lumbering vehicles were standing.

The bullocks were unyoked — boxes, barrels, sacks of flour and parcels of all sorts were strewn over the ground, or carried off into the verandah to be opened or stored away until needed. The bullock-drivers were put up for the night, and we were returning to our chairs and pipes once more, when a fresh commotion ensued.

This time it was the arrival of a strange-looking man on horseback, with three or four letter-bags slung round him.

"The mail. The mail!" cried the two girls. "But how late you are to-night, Dermot," added Janet. "I suppose you won't object to a nobbler, or are you going to put up here?"

I heard a voice with a strong Irish accent informing her that the speaker was bound for another station further up the river — and after due refreshment and some two minutes' rest and gossip he took himself off.

McKaye brought the mail-bag into the

27*

verandah and proceeded to open it.   He
handed the girls some newspapers and
magazines.   For himself there were two
letters.   I leant back in the low cane lounge,
smoking and watching the scene before me.
A lazy satisfied content was the only sensation
I experienced.   Everything was peaceful,
restful, quiet.   A soft cool wind brought a
delicious sense of coolness and exhilaration.
The full moon was shedding lustre over the
dark trees and rippling water, the acacias
and cactus gave forth a musky fragrance—an
orange tree laden with blossoms made the air
heavy with perfume.

I watched the brilliant belt of stars in the
clear dark blue of the sky.   The lustre of the
moonlight made a radiance strangely bright
and clear.   McKaye was able to read his
letters with no artificial aid of lamp or
candle.

Afterwards how all that scene came back
to me !   The restful calm, the scented air, the
lights and shadows and perfumes—even the
rustle of the paper as the girls cut the leaves

and their low laughter and exclamations as they turned over the illustrated pages.

An exclamation from the old Scotchman fell on my ears; I did not pay much attention to it. Presently he rose to his feet and folded the letters together and put them back in their envelopes.

"Good news, I hope," I said carelessly, as I glanced up at his tall wiry figure.

"Oh, yes," he answered. "I was only thinking it was somewhat odd I should have been speaking of the old home and the old friends to-night, and I've just had a letter from the Highland Laird I mentioned — Campbell his name is— Campbell of Corriemoor. He writes to say he's just been and got married. I thought he was a confirmed old bachelor. Well, well, there's no telling what folk may do."

I sat there, quite still, my eyes fixed on the curling smoke-wreaths.

"Campbell of Corriemoor?" I said at last my dry lips seeming to frame the words with difficulty. "I seem to know the name. Who has he married?"

"Quite a young lass, seemingly," said the old Scotchman. "A Miss Lindsay, who was staying on a visit with some Inverness folk. Well, I wish him luck and happiness. Matrimony is always more or less of a venture, especially when a man is getting on in years a bit, and the Laird's far from young now."

I made no observation. What could I say? Had I not always expected it— imagined it? Why should I care now? Voluntarily I had given her up, and exiled myself. Voluntarily thrown away her fresh young love, her tender, trustful girl's heart. If she had learnt to console herself—had accepted a worthier suitor, surely I could not blame her. Yet all the time I told myself this, my heart was heavy within me, and something baser and more selfish would whisper, "She might have waited—had she loved you she would have waited."

Now my dream was over for ever. She

had settled her future for herself, and in all probability I had long ago faded from her memory, or only crossed it as a dark shadow —something she regretted and would be glad to forget.

A voice roused me at last. It was that of Huel Penryth. With a start I looked up —we were alone there in the verandah. The Scotchman and his two daughters had gone within. I had been too absorbed to notice their departure.

"I have spoken to you three times. What are you dreaming about?" asked Huel.

"A youthful folly," I answered somewhat bitterly.

"You knew this girl then?" he said in those quiet even tones of his.

I started. "How do you know?" I asked.

"A deduction—that is all," he answered. "I happened to catch sight of your face when McKaye was telling you about his friend's marriage. It was somewhat self-betraying —then you relapsed into gloomy thought — heeding nothing, hearing nothing. I guessed there was something in the back-ground."

I was silent for a moment. I did not feel inclined for confidences. Huel smoked on, his eyes looking calmly and meditatively at the quiet beauty of the scene.

"It is a pity," he said presently, "that we are all bound to go through that phase of folly at one period or another. But it is the case. I have had mine, you have had yours. There is always a time in a man's life when he is peculiarly susceptible to the influence of women. We act and re-act on one another and give rise to the idea that we are absolutely necessary for mutual happiness. It is nonsense, men have no need of women. Our minds can stand alone, women only have a softening and enervating influence upon us. We *may* strengthen them and awake reason and intelligence—they to us give little or nothing that is useful, or stimulating."

"It is as well no woman hears your heresies," I said languidly. I felt in no mood for discussion or analysis. What mattered it to me now whether women were good or bad, fair or false? That current of life which had set in their direction, once warmly and freely, seemed to have grown chill and languid, and now was flowing into other channels.

" You think," said Huel, in answer to my remark, " that if they heard me they would combat my prejudices. Believe me, the day has gone by for that. I am young in years, but by experience and suffering I could out-number the lives of two ordinary men. I have learnt many hard truths, but the greatest truth is to learn to stand alone —to recognise self as the law of life and the law of all progress. Beat down all in your path—care naught for your fellows— cease to entangle yourself with responsibilities around, above, below you—and you will win all you set yourself to win. Sentiment softens and subdues—it is a leading rein, perpetually drawing one into side-paths; the man who turns aside loses time and energy. The battle is to the swift and strong."

" Rather a selfish theory, is it not ? " I remarked.

" All humanity is selfish. To cease to be so, it must cease to recognise its own importance or its own influence. We live, work, toil, endure, for self and sake of self, though we choose to call it ambition, pride or affection. No man ever did a good or great action for a fellow-man without some grain of self at the root of the apparent sacrifice or nobility of that action. Look even at martyrdom. It was an individual idea of eternal suffering to be avoided— eternal punishment to be escaped — that made men and women apparently heroic. They wanted to save their own souls, and they believed they were doing it. Impress upon a man's mind that the amputation of a limb will save his life, or a painful and disagreeable remedy prolong it, and he will adopt your cure. The spiritual side of his nature can be touched to equal heroism if

once he is convinced that he has a spirit,
and that for its benefit or gain he must
endure a brief martyrdom. The floods of
superstition flowed with wild and frantic
force over men's souls at certain periods of
their history. Calm thought or action was
made impossible, and mutual encouragement
rendered martyrdom a matter of necessity,
or cowardice. But it was always personal
salvation—and yet future gain—that were
of paramount importance. 'I must endure,'
'I must suffer,' 'I must be saved.' There
lay the real truth, though posterity has
glorified it with high-sounding words."

"You allow very little good in human
nature," I said, looking with wonder at his
flashing eyes, and pale, calm face.

"I think there is very little," he answered;
"and the greater the civilization the greater
the amount of vice. Our hypocrisy is
preposterous. If we lived up to one single
law of the religion we have set up—to one
single faith we profess—there would be no
crime, no injustice, no poverty and no

shame. But no one does live up to outward professions. The king on his throne—the cleric in his pulpit—the soldier who prates of glory — the patriot who pretends dis- interestedness — the merchant who trades with secret dishonesty—the law that is a crying disgrace to the justice it professes— each and all are but puppets of their own creation, strutting for their little space of time on their own stage—none daring to be true and honest to their own convictions, and therefore accepting the world as it is, and pretending that what it professes it performs. However, we are drifting a long way from our starting point. You have a sore heart to-night, my boy. Was this girl false to you? If so, be consoled that you learnt the truth early instead of late."

I shook my head.

"The fault was mine," I said. "I—I lost her. It is odd that now the loss is irre- vocable I should feel its sting so keenly."

"The wound touches your self-love," he

said cynically. "No man likes to feel he is readily or easily supplanted, even in a thing so light and capricious as a woman's fancy."

I rose abruptly.

"You are wrong," I said. "I was never worthy one thought of hers—never; but all the same——"

My voice broke—I could not speak—I could not tell him that for one wild, maddening moment, heart—soul—my whole being —longed with the vain longing of hopelessness to hold that little hand in mine once more, and hear that sweet, low voice say, "Douglas—I love you!"

CHAPTER V.

"Now conscience wakes despair
    That slumber'd—wakes the bitter memory
Of what was—what is—
        And what must be."

*   *   *   *   *   *

THE spring passed with swiftly-gliding step into the bloom and richness of summer. Huel Penryth and I were again at McKaye's station, having visited Sydney and Melbourne in the meantime. But neither of us took kindly to civilized life and its exactions and artifices after our wandering and erratic existence. We had accepted an invitation to spend Christmas with the McKayes, and accordingly the 24th of December found us there.

Great excitement prevailed in the family. It appeared that the girls had at last persuaded their father to take them to the

old country, and that they were to leave
early in the ensuing year.

They were full of it. We heard nothing
else discussed from morning till night. I
cannot remember when the first hint or
suggestion was thrown out that Huel and I
should accompany them, but gradually we
ceased to oppose or ridicule the idea, and
began to discuss its probability together.

We had plenty of money — we had no
ties to keep us here. The McKayes were
urgent, and — at last — I found myself
confessing that I would like to go back,
if only for a short time. I had heard no
news of my father since I left Scotland.
That, of course, was my own fault. I had
never written to anyone to relate my escape
from the wrecked vessel, and no doubt I was
believed to be drowned.

It amused me a little to picture the
astonishment and consternation that might
possibly ensue if I appeared in my birthplace
in the new and important aspect of a wealthy
man.

How readily my faults and escapades would be forgiven. How excusable they would look under the gilded cover of success. I laughed somewhat bitterly as I thought of it, and thought too, with a longing I hardly liked to acknowledge, of the girl whose soft eyes would once have given me so sweet a welcome.

Would she be much changed? Two years make a great difference in a girl's life—and marriage makes a greater.

Yet I could not picture her a woman. Always in my fancy she lived as the fairy-like fragile little being, whose wistful eyes had grown wet with tears when I had sung " Auld Robin Gray" that first night we met.

It annoyed me sometimes that I could not forget her, I had always found it so easy a matter to forget other women. And now, try as I might to convince myself I was going home for a hundred different reasons, *one* lurked at the bottom of all—unacknowledged, but known to my own heart; I wanted to see her again. I wanted to know if she was happy, if I was quite forgotten !

Whether the proceeding was unwise or not I did not argue. Once having consented to return, I felt a sense of relief at my own decision, and as Huel was still to be my companion I felt I was leaving nothing to regret behind me.

I had grown strongly attached to this strange man. Perhaps he was not a very safe or a very good companion for me, especially in the impressionable stage of my life, but he had a force and originality of character that I liked.

It seemed strange to me that he had not made a mark in the world, with his many gifts and brilliant qualities.

Perhaps that hidden spring of bitterness, cynicism, and disbelief had poisoned the sweeter currents of his nature, and now he took a morbid delight in denying all good in mankind, and upholding materialism as his god, and nature as his religion.

He had not alluded again to that secret of mine which he had guessed when I heard the news of Campbell of Corriemoor's marriage.

Only the night before we sailed he said abruptly, " Your home is near Inverness, is it not ? "

" Yes," I answered, wondering why he asked the question.

" And where is Corriemoor? " he continued, his eyes searching my face somewhat keenly.

" Oh," I said with indifference, " that is a long way from my part of the country. Indeed, I have never even seen it."

" You know its owner though ? "

" Oh, yes," I said. " But not intimately. He was a great personage, and I—a nobody."

" And he has married—married the girl whom you loved. I hope, for her sake, you will not meet." He spoke moodily—abstractedly. I looked at him in surprise. I felt the colour rising to my face.

" Why do you say that ? " I asked.

" Because I feel afraid of you, and because I once, long, long years ago, knew a man who, like you, threw away the treasure of a girl's love, and learnt, too late, the value of his loss."

"We are not likely to meet," I said coldly.
"Even if we were——"

"Ah," he said, with an odd flash in his
dark eyes, "do not say that. It argues self-
confidence, but not conviction. You have
carried a sore heart about with you for many
a long day. Your own folly may be to blame,
I daresay it is. But do not fancy any obstacle
or barrier that ever yet was set up, has acted
to men's passions as anything but an incentive.
Love may die a natural death of weariness or
disenchantment, but no power yet could kill
it out of the heart where it had no *right* to
live, and no hope of attainment. To love
greatly is to be very unhappy, and very
hopeless. What is refused to forgetfulness, is
only what man's vanity calls fidelity. Were
memory curable there would be no such
thing."

"It is useless to argue with such an un-
believer as you are, Huel," I said, somewhat
bitterly. "According to you, there is no
good in anything or anyone, no human
sentiment worthy of praise, and no genuine

28*

feeling in man or woman, save only their love of self."

"Well," he said coolly, "can you recall any historical or recorded instance of the 'divine passion,' which has not been celebrated for its unhappiness, peril, or tragedy? Commonplace affections I grant may sail smoothly along the sea of individual existence, but I speak of love—the divinest, subtlest, sweetest and most torturing of human passions. It is divine only so long as its object is surrounded by that halo of 'inaccessibility.' Stolen hours, silent dreams, impassioned longings, these alone invest it with the power to uplift our grosser natures. We cease to idealize when we are forced to live the dreary, commonplace of every day life with that ideal. Habit is the death of romance, and romance is the life of Love. The rose will not bloom when a slab of stone covers it. As the stone to the rose, so is the prose of accessibility to love."

"Then because this girl is lost to me by my own folly on the one side, by human laws of morality on the other, you fancy she will become doubly adorable?"

He shrugged his shoulders.

"The veriest Phyllis of the fields becomes a goddess in the eyes of the Corydon who cannot win her. Could he do so, her fair skin would be black and blue with bruises ere six months of matrimonial bliss had flown!"

"Heresy, rank heresy," I said, "there are plenty of happy marriages in all ranks and grades of life. Naturally one's feelings can't be always at high pressure. But to love with reverence, and sympathy, and perfect comprehension, is a very happy state of feeling."

"It is monotonous, and monotony is bound to become wearisome. Love has always been painted with wings, you cannot cage him without detriment to gailer or prisoner. Granted perfect liberty, passion may still be faithful. Absence, variety, even pain, will keep it alive far longer than success. The mistake of love is that it is almost always unequal. If the woman loves more deeply

than the man, she is exacting, jealous, un-
reasonable.   If, on the other hand, his passion
exceeds hers, he burdens her with equal
exactions and suspicions.   he repeats himself
ad nauseam, and she wearies.   Not the
sweetest song ever written but will pall by
daily repetition.   You will find I am right the
more you study human nature.   The scales
are almost always unevenly weighted, no two
natures are exactly balanced.   One is poor
and light, the other deep and strong.   One
capricious, the other steadfast.   One pro-
found, the other shallow.   One formed for
truth, the other wavering and unreliable.
For love to be equal, and that happens in one
case out of a million, there must be the
most perfect comprehension, the most ex-
quisite sympathy; there must be a likeness,
yet a subtle variation, between both natures,
a charm which both recognise and are wise
enough to preserve without attempting to
analyse its secret."

"But most people are commonplace, to
use your own words, and all this perfection of

sentiment and feeling would be unnecessary and undesired," I said.

"Then let no one blame inconstancy," he answered quickly. "It is the natural result of an attempt to chain sentiment into the dull and heavy harness of every-day life. Here and there it breaks loose, and runs recklessly into a new path of its own. There are plenty of people who win love, but cannot keep it, indeed, do not even trouble themselves to make the effort. Yet those are the persons who make the greatest outcry about morality."

"What would you do?" I asked. "If—if anyone you loved very dearly were false to you? Could you philosophize so readily then over broken vows, and falsified honour?"

I fancied his face grew a shade paler, his lips set themselves into a hard, stern line.

"I hope," he said, "that I should have strength of mind sufficient to recognize the uselessness of reproach or regret. What one cannot hold securely, one must expect to lose. If a man thinks himself too secure of a woman's affection, he is apt to undervalue it, or she believes that he does. He makes the mistake of over-worshipping her, in the first stage of his love, and neglecting her, in proof of his trust, in the second. The third stage is generally a sudden awaking on his part to find he has lost what he fancied to be securely his own. Rebellion is useless. You cannot force back an affection into the old channels, you cannot raise fire from dead ashes. What use to try? I would not, for my part, raise a finger to win back a woman who had once shown me she had ceased to love. Let her go. If she finds herself the worse for her unfaith, she must suffer for it. Fate is inexorable. We make our own punishment, by our own misdeeds. No need to rail and storm at the weak human element which assists us to do both.

"What made you such a philosopher, Huel?" I asked suddenly.

He shrugged his shoulders. "Observation, suffering, and necessity. How old should you think me, Douglas?"

I looked scrutinizingly at the calm face, the worn, lined brow, the dark, inscrutable eyes, the thick waves of hair tossed so carelessly back above the leonine head.

"About thirty-five," I answered.

He smiled. "No, I am forty-two in actual years, a hundred by experience and sorrow. Some day, perhaps, I will tell you my story. I have never breathed it to mortal yet. Confidence is a feminine attribute. Men can exist, and be perfect friends and companions, yet never exchange one secret of their lives. Is that not true?"

"Perfectly true. I suppose we are enough for each other, without going into the background of previous events. Perhaps we are less exacting than women in friendship as in love."

He was silent. I saw the well-known look of gloomy absorption gather in his strange eyes. His memory had wandered back no doubt to that "background" whose shadows had darkened his life for many weary years.

I had learnt by this time to understand his moods and respect his silence.

I said no more then. But my curiosity was awakened more keenly than it had ever been.

What sorrow had so altered his nature and turned it to bitterness and hardness? What secret lay at the root of his apparent coldness and cynicism—his disbelief in all the softer or purer emotions that to most men make up the sum of life?

Had a woman's hand dealt the blow which had turned youth to age, and all the fresh, sweet currents of life to gall and bitterness?

Some day, perhaps, I should know.

CHAPTER VI.

THE WEB OF FATE.

> "—And reason'd high
> Of Providence—foreknowledge—will and fate—
> Fix'd fate—free will—foreknowledge absolute,
> And found no end, in wond'ring mazes lost.
>   *   *   *   *   *   *
> Our torments also may in length of time
> Become our elements."

Of the voyage and its incidents there is no need to speak. It was monotonous and fairly pleasant.

I could scarcely believe that two years had passed since I had travelled those same seas and gazed on those same scenes. Two years! They seemed like twenty.

As we drew nearer and nearer to our destination, a strange nervousness overtook me. I avoided the McKayes, I could not bear the light chatter and incessant curious questioning of the girls. Even Huel's companionship irritated me.

When the steamer reached Liverpool we separated. The McKayes were going first to London, but Huel and I had determined to travel on to Scotland at once.

We rested at Edinburgh and I telegraphed from there to my father, informing him of my speedy arrival. I knew him well enough to feel assured the news would not excite or please him. I wondered whether he had believed me dead all. this time. It was while at Edinburgh that the first thought of Mrs. Dunleith flashed into my mind. Should I call and see whether she was at her old address? After all, I owed her some such attention, considering her interest in me and the terms on which we had parted.

After dinner, that night of our arrival, I asked Huel Penryth's advice on the subject, telling him frankly how matters had been between her and myself, and that she had furnished me with those letters of introduction to the people in Canada which I had lost in the shipwreck.

"I think it would be only polite of you to

call," he said. "Suppose we stroll round there to-night? It is not a conventional hour for visiting, but possibly she will excuse that."

"I hardly think she will be in Edinburgh," I said. "Most probably she has left, or is travelling about, she never cared to stay long in one place. However, we will go and see for ourselves. You must come in and see her," I added. "I should like you to meet, she is a woman who has always puzzled me a good deal. I fancy she has had a very unhappy past. She is reckless, but not bad. A very kind-hearted woman, but liable, I should say, to be led aside by impulse. Not a favourite with her own sex at all."

"I would rather not see her," he said. "I am no friend to the sex, as you know, and a woman of her type would be particularly obnoxious to me."

"But as a favour to me, Huel," I urged.

He flashed a keen glance at me. "Are you afraid of a *tête-à-tête?*" he said. "Well, a third person is decidedly a barrier to sentiment. But it will be trying, will it not?"

I laughed. "For me—no. I had never any sentiment, as you call it, for her. She was one of those women who could be very good company to a man, smoke, drink, laugh and jest, all *en bon camarade*, but that was all."

"A widow, you said?"

"Yes. I never heard her say so, but indirectly she always led me to believe it."

"I think you were fortunate in escaping an entanglement," he said abruptly. "She is the type of woman to be dangerous, where her passions are concerned."

"Oh, there was nothing so serious as that," I said lightly. "Her fancy for me was but a very light and passing one. Besides, I was a mere boy, years and years younger than herself."

"And you have not written, or held any communication with her since you left her two years ago?"

" No.   Do you think it advisable to resume the acquaintance ? "

He shook his head doubtfully.

" I will go with you," he said, at last, " and I will see her before answering that question."

*   *   *   *   *

The moon was shining brilliantly over the picturesque extent of Princes Street, as we left the hotel and turned in the direction that had once been s) familiar to me.

Huel Penryth stood silent for a moment, contemplating the scene with grave admiration.

" One has read of it so often," he said, " I must confess to being a little disappointed when I first saw it.   But now it is deserving of all the praise lavished upon it.   What a marvellous alchemist is moonlight."

Indeed the scene was very beautiful.   The gardens, sloping to the bottom of the valley, were full of lights and shadows.   The opposite heights, crowned with the quaint houses of the Old Town, lost all the ugliness and gloom

which the day's cruel candour would so
plainly reveal. The famous Castle towered
above on its rocky perch, every turret and
tower standing out distinctly in the pale,
clear light.

"Most feudal castles are alike," said Huel,
as we walked on, "but I grant this one of
your capital is unique in its position. You
have a background of park, hills, sea—and at
your feet a town modern as the veriest
Philistine could desire. Certainly it is very
beautiful. I suppose you feel a Scotchman's
pride in it all. For my part I never could
see why the mere fact of being born in a
place invests it with a halo of superiority over
all other places."

"Not superiority—only a deeper interest
or attachment," I said.

He shrugged his shoulders.

"Well, I am too cosmopolitan for that, I
fear. I suppose few places in the old country
are more wildly and grandly beautiful than
my old home on the Cornish coast, and yet I
never care to re-visit it."

We were opposite the Royal Institution with its graceful twin structure, the National Gallery, breaking the sweep of the public gardens. How long ago it seemed to me since I had seen them. A strange chill touched my heart as involuntarily I paused and looked at them once more. A sense of impending trouble or misfortune, for which I could not account, laid its cold pressure on brain and nerve, and seemed to warn me against the errand on which I was bent.

I shook off the feeling with an effort. "Come—let us go," I said. "I am afraid we are very late for a call as it is."

* * * * *

Mrs. Dunleith had rented a furnished flat when I was last in Edinburgh. Thither we now bent our steps. We toiled up the cold, white, general staircase, and rang at the third floor.

The servant announced that Mrs. Dunleith was staying there, and was at home.

She conducted us into a small ante-room,

and left us there while she went to inform her mistress of my name.

Ere a moment had passed, I heard an eager voice, the rustle of feminine skirts, then the door was thrown hurriedly open. A vision in pale amber silk, clinging in soft folds to the lissom, slender figure—dark eyes, eager, lustrous—white hands outstretched, a well-known voice. "Douglas!—can it really be you?" Then——

It was not my figure that rose to welcome her, it was not my face that turned her bright and eager one to cold, grey, death-like horror. It was not word or voice of mine that with one single word cut short her greeting. No, it was Huel Penryth's. Swift as thought he had sprung forward and faced her, and she— meeting his gaze—seemed frozen into stony terror. I saw her shiver and recoil—I heard the low gasp of fear from her white lips. Then she staggered blindly forward, and fell almost at my feet—senseless.

I raised her hurriedly, and laid her on the couch.

Huel stood there motionless—his arms folded, his dark face set in hard and cruel lines.

"What is it?" I cried in astonishment. "Do you know her?"

He looked steadily at the motionless figure, the white face, the closed eyes.

"To my bitter cost," he said.

*   *   *   *   *

CHAPTER VII.

A DISCOVERY.

> " Then black despair,
> The shadow of a starless night, was thrown
> Over the world in which I moved alone."

I HAD never seen on the face of any human being such an expression of hatred and contempt as that which flashed over Huel Penryth's usually calm, grave features.

I stood there silent and dismayed, as one feels in presence of some great tragedy.

That he should have come from the end of the earth to meet the woman who had made life bitter to his youth!

Truly Fate works strangely!

I looked from him to the white face and senseless form on the couch. Neither of us had made any effort to restore her senses.

I was too startled, and he—I imagined—too embittered.

" What shall I do ? " I said, at last. " Ring
for her maid ? Do you wish to stay ? "

"I must speak to her," he said abruptly.
" But, for her own sake, spare her the humiliation of your presence. Wait for me in the
street below. I shall not detain you long."

I gave one more glance at that still and
motionless figure, and then left them together.

Outside in the quiet street I paced to and
fro for a very long time. My thoughts were
busy with conjectures. All the bitter
speeches, the cruel truths, the unsparing
sarcasms hurled at the sins and frailties of
women by Huel Penryth, came back to my
mind. And this woman was the cause.

Involuntarily I traced back my own
acquaintance with her. With calmer brain
and more critical judgment than my hot
youth had known, I went step by step along
that path of seeming triviality which had
ended now so strangely.

I remembered the subtle hints, the little
bursts of mocking laughter — the fanciful
caprices—the faint jealousies—the thousand

and one arts and witcheries which this woman had used so unsparingly.

She had hated Athole Lindsay from the first, and I remembered the girl's same instinct about her—strange that women are so keen, and detect a rival where a man's coarser nature sees no harm or danger.

A thousand things that she had said or insinuated respecting youthful love, boyish infatuation, the folly and imprudence of long engagements, the selfishness of early claims in face of more advantageous alliances— those spider-threads of mischief and malice which I could have once brushed away so easily, but which I had foolishly allowed to weave their web of entanglement and mis- understanding about me — all these came crowding back to my memory as I paced to and fro in the quiet moonlight.

Above my head the stars shone in the soft blue arc of the heavens. The solemn beauty, the intense stillness, seemed a rebuke to the stormy passions and cruel feuds of men. I wondered what was passing between those two in the room above. Did Huel Penryth hide some brute element of jealousy and savagery beneath that calm exterior. The look that had flashed over his face when he saw Dora Dunleith, had startled me by its revelation of fury and pent-up hatred. In that instant the man's inner nature seemed to flash out in a rebellion against long years of repression and restraint. The torments of a soul whose yearnings and faith had been pierced through and through by some sword of anguish, had burst forth at last into outward expression.

I felt sorry for the woman, who would wake from her sleep of unconsciousness, and face at last the retribution of garnered years.

Sorry, and somewhat afraid too, though I well knew Huel's extraordinary power of self-restraint.

How long he was—how long. He had told me to wait but a few minutes, and already half an hour had passed and there was no sign of him.

*   *   *   *   *

Another quarter of an hour, and still I kept my lonely vigil in that street, and still Huel did not appear.

Wearied and disturbed I had almost resolved on returning to the hotel, when at last he made his appearance.

I went eagerly forward but the look on his face hushed the question on my lips. Its white savagery, the gleam of the dark eyes, the set fierce sternness of the mouth, all spoke a tale of passion and wrath more plainly than any words.

He walked along by my side apparently unconscious of my presence. From time to time his lips moved. Strange disjointed words fell from them.

"When a mortal delivers himself to the Powers of Darkness he yields the citadel of his being to the guard of its direst foes . . I made the compact ; to-night might have set its seal . . Why did I hesitate? Are those who rob human life less murderous than those who steal from mind and soul their youth, and faith, and purity . . .

Avenge the evil they say to me—But how?
Shall I take the life that is at my mercy, or
spare it for further ill doing . . . Chaos,
storm, darkness—my soul is engulfed in the
maelström of its own passions. The voices
I hear to-night are only those of fiends and
tempters. . ."

"Huel," I said entreatingly, and laid my
hand on his arm. He stopped and faced me
abruptly. "Is it you, Douglas?" he muttered in a confused, dull manner.

I drew him into the quiet gardens and, still
keeping my hold of his arm, besought him to
calm himself. He lifted his hat and shook
back the dark waves of hair from his brow
with an impatient gesture.

"Calm—peace," he muttered, "they are
not for me. The moral harmony of my
nature has long been turned to discord. I
believe no good of man or woman—to-night
a murderer's soul is all that is left to me . .
all—all!"

"You—oh, God grant you have not killed
the woman," I faltered in accents of horror.

The mockery of his harsh laughter fell on the still night air.

"My hands were at her throat," he said. "I saw the black marks on the fair white skin that once in youth's madness I had kissed with love's wild rapture. . . . God! what fools men are? When shall we cease to deify those fair images of beauty, unknowing the whited sepulchres they are. Human animals, creatures of prey, hiding under supple skin and velvet sheath the treachery that springs on its victim, the tiger-claws that wound them to the death. Like tiger and serpent they ravage and destroy, and like animal and reptile they know no pity and suffer no remorse!"

I let him rave on. I felt bewildered and alarmed at the sudden change in the cold self-controlled being I had known so long. His wrath lived less in the spoken words he muttered than in the frenzied gleam of his flashing eyes, those portals to his strange nature, in the utter uprooting of all the strength and calmness that had so characterized his face.

I walked silently beside him, reflecting with some irony on the uselessness of man's philosophy until he can assure himself he is utterly and entirely separated from earthly ties. Sorrow, treachery, misfortune will always find human soil for the sowing of their inexhaustible seed. He, the cold dead tree of human life, proud of that very deadness and vaunting its inability to put forth again one single shoot of love or faith or human desire, had yet regained through suffering the power of feeling—had not, even through years of abstinence and indifference learnt to break those fibres of passion and pride which bind one nature to another, and connect their lives, actions and desires with the intimacy of mutual interest and association.

*　　*　　*　　*　　*

"Where are we?" cried Huel Penryth, suddenly starting as one in a dream.

So absorbed had we been in our thoughts and emotions that neither of us had paid much heed to where our footsteps wandered.

When he spoke we were standing on the summit of Arthur's Seat, looking down from its height on the beautiful city below. The white splendour of the moonlight fell over dark Holyrood and the grim and dusky buildings of the Old Town. To the southeast the loch of Duddingston gleamed like a silver mirror, and the little village itself lay hushed and calm in the peace of the quiet night. The ruins of St. Anthony's Chapel stood out bold and clear on the broad shoulder of the hill. The sound of the water rushing from its spring in the rock behind the hermit's cell, was the only sound that disturbed the stillness.

We stood there and contemplated the scene for long, neither of us speaking. At last Huel turned to me—a deep sigh almost a groan burst from his lips.

" Nature rebukes me," he said, his voice shaken and softened by intense feeling. " I hear her. . . I am calm once more. After all my lessons, after all my boasts, to think that I could be moved to such a

display of evil feelings and vengeful desires!
But it is over now. . . The storm rages in
a higher sphere, apart from physical wrath
and vengeance. It is in my brain. . . A
field of destroyed faith and dispelled illusions.
I set myself apart from humanity long long
ago. Why did I suffer the memory of past
wrongs to sting feeling to life again? . . .
It was the struggle of philosophy against
despair; no excuse, no reason, no argument.
I have declared man to be master of Nature
and master of himself. . . Alas! how
weak he proves when trial comes!"

He folded his arms across his chest. His
head sank as if in sudden self-abasement.
Wonderingly I had followed him through
every phase of every changing mood, waiting
patiently till passion should have exhausted
itself — as, fortunately for humanity, all
strong emotions must exhaust themselves
in course of time. His face looked deadly
pale as the moon-rays fell on it. The
reaction of feeling centred itself now in a
strange, almost pathetic humility of expres-

sion, the humility of a great strength finding itself but a great weakness.

He who had ridiculed feeling as childish, and anger as unphilosophical, had now experienced each emotion in turn and abandoned himself to their sway unresistingly.

He lifted his white face at last, and it looked almost unearthly in its solemn calm.

"It was Destiny," he said. "It could not be avoided. Listen, Douglas — for the first time in my life I unseal my lips and give their secret to another. Perhaps, had your fate not linked itself with mine, your hand not led me to her presence, I should have never spoken these words. Seal them into silence, respect the weakness that made its vaunt so triumphantly, only to know itself the sport and slave of temptation after all."

He drew me down on the rough stone beside which we stood, and there in the midnight solitude of the hermit's hill, I heard the story of wasted passion and wilful wrong that had laid waste this strange man's life.

CHAPTER VIII.

" A love that took an early root,
　And had an early doom."

"　.　.　.　.　　Deep as love,
　Deep as first love, and wild with all regret ;
　O death in life! the days that are no more."

" I HAVE told you I am a native of Cornwall.
For a century back my people were born,
lived, and died there. My earliest recollections are of a sea-coast, wild in its grandeur,
and as terrible in storm as it was beautiful in
its serene peace and stillness. My father was
owner of some great slate quarries and mines,
and was accounted a person of great importance. I had no brothers or sisters; my
childhood was a somewhat lonely one. To
this fact I owe, perhaps, a tendency to
romance and a passion for solitude. All
around me fostered such feelings. The

legends of the country, the wildly picturesque surroundings, the never-ending beauty
of combe and cave and valley and height,
and the storied lore of Tintagel, whither I
loved to wander and dream whole days away.
My father I seldom saw; my mother had
been an invalid from my birth. My educa-
tion was carried on in a somewhat desultory
fashion. I went to school three or four days
in the week. In the winter, when the
weather was bad, I stayed at home engrossed with my books. I read much and at
random. There was no one to heed or direct
me. When I was about fourteen, a relation
of my father's came to live with us, a strange
and eccentric being, old, bent, bowed down
with infirmities of age, but with an intellect
vigorous and keen as it was subtle and
dangerous. He attracted me strangely, and
despite the vast difference in our years, he
showed a greater preference for my society
than for that of any other inmate of our
household. To this man I owe an extraordinary amount of knowledge that I could

not have acquired at that time from any routine of teaching. He had been a student of Nature, a professor of astrology, knew something on all subjects connected with physical science, and possessed a vast store of occult lore that terrified while it allured me into following its mythical speculations, and weird theories. Amidst such surroundings, and under such influences, it is not to be wondered at that I was somewhat different to most youths of sixteen. At this time I had my first grave difference with my father. He was naturally anxious that I should make myself acquainted with the details of his business, but I had an extreme aversion to the dull mechanical routine, the noisy machinery — the splitting, trimming and polishing of the great blocks, yielded by the slate quarry. To me it was all hideous, noisy, repugnant. I had seen the works often from my very earliest childhood. The great rock rent and torn asunder for sake of its unexhausted hoards; the engines and cables, and various machines for carrying the

materials to the heights above. The yawning
depths of the pit, the immense masses of
débris piled together, and left as useless after
the labour of years, all those inventions by
which Man wrested the spoils of Nature from
her breast, and turned peace and beauty to
noise and turmoil and hideousness for sake of
his own gain, were familiar enough to me.
When my father made the discovery that I
was old enough to learn something of the
business, to which he and his father before
him owed their wealth and importance, I
gave him to understand, that I would as soon
pass my days in a torture-chamber. At first
he was astonished, then indignant, and finally
gave me to understand that I should have
one year more of ' idleness,' as he called it,
in which to make up my mind and acquaint
myself with the works and their management
—if, at the expiration of that period, I still
determined to have nothing to do with the
business, he should adopt a distant relative
and give him the place intended for me, and I
might go out into the world and seek my

own fortune, unaided by the wealth or
influence I had voluntarily forfeited. It was
an arbitrary decision, but then the world tells
us that the fact of parentage is to many
minds only a reason for tyranny and moral
oppression; as if the fact of begetting the
body gave any right to rule or coerce the
mind! *That*, at least, is an independent
heritage. None may shape or form it. None
may decide its bent or inclination. It is not
man's gift, and, therefore, not under man's
control. I tried to make my father understand this, but he simply grew enraged at my
audacity, and would not listen to my argu-
ments."

"Our cases are not unlike," I said, as Huel
paused in his narrative. "Though I must
confess you present the duty of parent and
child in a novel light. As you say, the *fact*
of parentage seems to have always been a
sufficient reason for both mental and physical
rule. Body and mind are expected to be in
equal subjection, even to the most irrational
tyranny."

"But if you reflect on the subject," he said, "you cannot help seeing how young minds diverge from rule or pattern set before them. How a child develops talents, abilities, inclinations, totally at variance with those of its physical procreators. If the mind, temper and inclination were inherited in the same way as feature, form and colouring, every family would keep on reproducing itself to monotony. But very little observation points out the wide difference between the mind and the body that we suppose to be dual gifts of heredity. Indeed, were it not the sole effort of years of discipline and coercion when we are in the malleable state, to make us resemble our parents, we should be even less of 'copies' than we are."

"I think you are right," I said, thoughtfully; "but," I added, laughing in spite of myself, "what a revolution your views would create in all well-governed orthodox households. Why, there would be no such thing as discipline."

"I beg your pardon. There would be a

much wiser and more beneficent form of
discipline; one that recognised diversity of
character and honoured genius, that strength-
ened weakness and guided strength—that no
longer pursued that same form of rule for
each member of the family, but had the
sense to discriminate between them, and to
know that mental gifts and character are the
result of some mysterious force working from
the root and resistless in its work—not the
mere accident of birth and surroundings.
But I am diverging.   I have traced back
this page of my boyhood to give you some
idea of how my youth was affected by its
surroundings.   I come now to this pro-
bationary year appointed by my father, a
year destined to stand out for ever in my life
with its records of joy, woe, shame and
suffering.   Love, the love of youth, is a magic
wand, striking water from the rocks of the
hardest and most prosaic surroundings,
turning the darkest and driest soil into a
flower garden of beauty and promise. I—
fostered on romance, with little knowledge of

the realities of life, with passionate and uncomprehended cravings for the beautful, the imagined, the unknown—I—I met youth's common fate and with youth's common folly accepted it as a divine gift. I loved. How we met, who she was, whence she came, matters not. She had all her sex's cunning and coquetry. But to me she was Hebe in her virginal youth, Psyche in her beauty and grace; she was only a passing visitant, a being, so it seemed to me, from another and more glorious sphere, content to pause in this desolate region, and glorify it with such grace and loveliness as I had dimly dreamt of.

We met, by dawn, by night, in hours of sunrise and moonrise, by wild heights and in fern-haunted coves, dusky with sombre shade of oak and beech, sweet with sounds of ever-murmuring water. Who knows my land at all, knows well those silver trickling rills whose ceaseless music gladdens the summer's day, and the tender dreamy stillness of the night. I show her every fairy cove I knew so well, carpeted by white and shell-stewn

sands, beautiful with wonders of sea and
shore — worthy to be haunted by mermaids
of fabled beauty—though indeed it seemed
to me that never maid of land or sea was
worthy to compare with that radiant and
gracious presence which made all my life's
glory and delight .   .   .

"Oh, Youth! how we laugh at its follies in
the latter-day wisdom that trial and disillusion
and experience only too surely bring; yet
how in our heart of hearts we envy its pure
dreams and glorified faiths, which once lost
can never be regained through all life's span
of years! .   .   .   Well, I drank my cup of
folly to the dregs. My dream became reality
—I loved her, wooed her, won her—rising
heavenwards in varying moods of trans-
cendant bliss. I confided my secret to one
person only—the strange old being who had
been so dangerous a teacher. He was not
sympathetic—age seldom is—such age as his
could only look upon my rapturous ex-
pressions as blossoms of an exuberant fancy,
destined to fall soon enough from the tree that

was so proud of bearing them. In a way he was our friend, and my father being at this time absent from home, I took advantage of the fact to travel to Launceston, and there was married to Dorothy Tolverne. She was supposed to be there on a visit to some old school-mate. Indeed, long afterwards—when I was cool enough and rational enough to remember facts and circumstances — I recollected that it was she who made most of the arrangements, and planned with consummate skill, and secrecy, and assurance the whole details of the elopement. The next thing was to break the news to my father, and this my old friend had promised to do. A few weeks drifted by. I was too happy to heed the passage of time or trouble my head about my father's silence. My wife often questioned me as to his wealth and my position with regard to it. She seemed certain that he would forgive us, and that she would return to Penryth and queen it there as one of the richest and most important members of Cornish society. Her pretty airs and graces amused me. I had no social ambition and little regard for wealth. The old mansion, grey with age, and with its ivy-crowned tower and porch, with its quaint gateway and gardens, was dearer to me from history and association than from any importance it might possess in the eyes of the neighbourhood. But Dorothy held different views.

" At last the long expected letter from my father arrived. Whatever my fears or anticipations might have been, the reality far exceeded them. A few stern, curt lines conveyed to me the information that he considered my conduct in the light of an unpardonable affront. That as we were both under age, and had married without parents' consent, and by means of false representations, our union was not legal and he refused to consider it as such. If I would come to 'my senses,' give up this girl—beneath me as she was in birth and station—accept his offer of a place in the works, and return home in a penitent and proper frame of mind, he would consent to receive me. Failing to do this, we were to be strangers henceforth, and under no circumstances would he assist me or acknowledge me. I was aghast when I read this letter. I knew I was wholly dependent on my father, and I had not expected him to be so severe upon me. Silently I handed the letter to Dorothy. She perused it, her face changing from red to white as she took in its cold, unsparing insults.

"Then came a scene for which I was totally unprepared. Tears, reproaches, accusations followed sharp and swift. She accused me of purposely deceiving her; she had imagined I was rich, my position secure, and now she learnt that I was absolutely penniless and dependent. She said other things, too, more cruel and painful to bear, but I tried to excuse them in her natural indignation.

"Well, I am not going to dwell upon this time or the events that followed sharp and swift as stroke of cleaver. My castle of cards soon fell about my ears.

"Two months dragged along, embittered by my wife's growing coldness and unconcealed dislike. Our small stock of money was exhausted. I tried to get employment, but the remuneration was wretched and the work most unpalatable. Then, at the end of those two months, I learnt that the wife I had so adored was not only indifferent but false to me. Without hint or warning she left me one day, in the company of a military man, who had been staying for a short time at Launceston with his regiment. She wrote a brief note stating her intentions, and declaring that she had never considered herself legally married to me since she had read my father's letter. The best thing I could do was to set her free—if I had any doubts as to my claim on her—and then return home and make it up with my people. She was madly in love with this officer, and he intended to marry her as soon as I gave her up and freed her by law, which I could easily do. . . .

"That is all my story now, Douglas—the bald, hard facts. The woman I met in your presence to-night is the woman who wrecked

my youth and made sport of all its promises
and hopes. She is only an adventuress now,
and a dangerous one. She says her lover left
her two years after her elopement. A few
years later, she married an old and very
wealthy merchant, who died and left her all
his money. I told her that the marriage was
illegal, and have left her in terror as to
whether I am going to proceed against her
for bigamy. It is a poor revenge after all,
but when a man's lower passions are aroused
he is but a mean and craven thing; all loftier
instincts sink into that abyss of fierce anger,
broken pride, outraged honour. I wonder I
did not kill her!"

His voice had sunk into muttered and dis-
cordant tones; his face looked dark and evil
in the white moonlight. Abruptly he rose
and swept the thick, dark hair from off his
brow with an impatient gesture.

"Come," he said, "let us leave this place.
I cast her out of my heart long ago—it
cannot be more difficult to cast her out of my
memory now!"

CHAPTER IX.

" Oft in the stilly night,
 Ere slumber's chain has bound me,
Fond memory brings the light
 Of other days around me ;
  The smiles, the tears
  Of boyhood's years,
The words of love then spoken."

THE next day, we left Edinburgh and set out
for the Highlands. Huel had, to all appearance, recovered his composure, and was
outwardly the same calm, impassive being
I had so long known.

He spoke no word of the events of the past
night, nor did I allude to them We had the
carriage to ourselves, and smoked all the
way, now and then exchanging a remark as
to the scenery ; but even Killiecrankie's
famous pass evoked no enthusiasm in my
companion's mind, and the long, bleak chain

of the Grampians he called " a hideous desolation."

The afternoon was closing in when we reached Inverness and drove straight to an hotel. Mindful of my father's peculiarities, I deemed it wiser not to seek hospitality for myself and my friend at his hands. After some refreshment, I proposed to Huel that we should walk over and see the old man, and he consented at once.

The evening was chilly and gloomy, with a damp raw mist stealing up from the river, and the little town did not look its best.

Huel shivered as he crossed the bridge and looked back.

" I am not impressed with your climate, Douglas," he said; "it is depressing in the extreme."

" You are not fortunate in your present experience," I said. " But we certainly do have a great deal of rain and mist up here; it comes of being so near the hills, I suppose."

I felt somewhat melancholy and depressed,

myself. Every step was fraught with recollections. It seemed to me so long ago since those boyish days when I had lived here. So long ago since I had walked beside the river with Athole Lindsay — so long since that parting, when the little proud, hurt face had looked so coldly back to mine, and the forgiveness for which I pleaded had been withheld.

My thoughts would return to her, try as I might to rebel against their thraldom. Was she happy in her new life I wondered? Could she really care for one so cold and staid, and so much older than herself as was the Laird of Corriemoor?

In some selfish unworthy manner I almost hoped she was not happy. I kept telling myself that if she had but waited I should have come back to her, repentant, wiser, more worthy of her love than was the hot-headed boy she had known three years ago. My heart felt strangely sore and troubled as one after another came the familiar landmarks. There dark *Tom-na-Hurich* frowned

in the dim light, and westwards again, Craig
Phadric towered in solitary grandeur, and
fields, and meadows, and woods met my eyes
once more, unchanged save for the difference
of season.

The mist lifted slightly as we reached the
open country, and faint gleams of starlight
showed at intervals between rifts of parted
clouds.

"You are very silent," said Huel Penryth.
"Where are your thoughts? I need not
ask though. I am no stranger to the pain
of recalled memories."

"Yes," I said. "I was back in the past.
One wonders that Time plays such strange
tricks with one. Away from here, those two
years seemed a lifetime—now, I could
believe it was only yesterday I stood here
and watched the sun setting over that hill
yonder."

"Do you intend staying long in Scotland?"
he asked presently, "because if not, you
might come with me to my Cornish home. I
have not re-visited it since I left."

" Was your father reconciled to you ? " I asked with some hesitation.

He shook his head. " No, and he died very suddenly, before he had time to alter his will, so I inherited everything. I put the whole business into the hands of a manager, a man who understood it, and on whom I knew I could depend. I have never been near the place since. I suppose I am what the world calls ' wealthy,' but I prefer my wandering life to any routine of civilization."

" Some day," I said, " you will grow tired of it."

He shook his head. " I think not. There is something Bohemian in my nature. I dislike all conventionality. Besides, I could not endure the boredom and narrow-mindedness of English country life. The perpetual gossip and tittle-tattle, the prying into and interference with one's affairs. I never could understand why, in small towns, people take such an overpowering interest in all one does and says. Things that don't concern them in the very least."

I laughed somewhat bitterly. The days were not so long past since I had suffered from back-biting tongues and impertinent interference, garbed in kindly interest, and as such, hiding, or seeming to hide, their barbed insults.

"Oh," I said, "if it were only 'interest,' one might find excuse, but it is the amount of conjecture and falseness, that is so trying."

He shrugged his shoulders with the old petulant gesture I knew so well.

"It is a wild field," he said. "First, curiosity and self-importance lead the way; then come suggestions, hints, surmises, tending to conclusions, probable, but not actual, and decisions more or less uncharitable. Yet what cobwebs they are in reality, idle threads spun from idleness, flippancy, ill-nature, as the case may be. But they carry their sting, none the less."

"It is strange," I said, "how cruelly one human being will stab another to the heart with an idle or unkind word. Yet that same individual would shrink from inflicting bodily pain, even on a dumb animal."

"We are odd compounds of cruelty and kindness," said Huel. "And it is the blundering of fools that too often makes a wise man's suffering. Strange, but true. When you look out on life from a field of experience and sorrow, you can afford to smile at the follies, but in their day they have hurt you and the pain is hard to forget."

Then we relapsed into silence—each busied with his own thoughts and reflections, until we reached my father's house.

*   *   *   *   *

Not a ray of light greeted us from the old building of grey stone, standing solitary and grim in its neglected garden.

I knocked at the front door, which, after some delay, was opened by old Janet. She held a candle in her hand, which flickered wildly in the draught and threw strange shadows on her old, withered face and frilled cap-border, and the patched and darned black gown she wore.

"Well, Janet," I said cheerily, "you see

31*

I've come back again. How are you and how is my father? Is he in?"

She drew back into the gloomy little hall, and set down her candle.

"So it's yoursel', Mister Douglas," she said. "Are ye no fair out o' your wits to come here at sic' an hour o' nicht. Your fayther's in, of course he's in, but he's nae sitting up. He's been in bed this hour and mair."

"Well, I suppose I can see him," I said, "and my friend can step into the parlour."

I walked in, taking up the candle as I did so, and old Janet hobbled after me.

"You won't have a very lofty idea of Scotch hospitality," I said, as we entered the dark and fireless parlour. How indescribably dismal and desolate it looked. The old worn horse-hair chairs set in stiff array against the faded paper of the walls, the dingy table-cover on the square table, the bookcase in the recess by the fire-place. All were unchanged, save by the two years' passage of time which lay between me and my last look at them.

"Fetch another candle, Janet," I said, and the old woman, muttering and grumbling, hobbled away to obey me.

Huel glanced around. He made no remark, nor did I. Perhaps he was tracing back in his mind the influences and surroundings of my youth, and wondering whether to pity or praise them for the character they had served to mould.

As for myself, there was a curious mingling of repulsion and indifference in my heart as I looked at those miserly records of the past.

How unhappy I had been here once. How passionately I had rebelled — suffered — struggled against the tyranny that bound me so hopelessly. Well, it was something to know I had shaken it off at last—that I could face my father in my new-born independence of manhood and tell him I had for ever escaped that thraldom of unhappy youth, and desired or asked nothing of any man in future.

At this moment Janet returned with another candle and the information that my father was awake, and would see me if I would step up into his bedroom.

With a hasty apology to Huel, who was examining the volumes in the book-case, I went upstairs.

The old man was sitting up in bed, his grey hairs covered with an old woollen night-cap, his lean yellow hands clasping and unclasping themselves nervously as was his wont when agitated.

We shook hands in our usual unemotional manner.

"I did not expect you to-night," he said, looking at me keenly from under his bushy grey eyebrows. "You've no come to stay, I hope, there's nae room ready for ye, and Janet, she's no fit to set to work at this hour and prepare food."

"Pray don't trouble," I answered. "I'm staying at an hotel in Inverness with a friend. I hadn't the least intention of burdening you with my presence."

He drew a breath of relief. "Ah, well, you've grown mair considerate than ye used

to be.   And so you've been nigh shipwrecked
and have met with manifold disasters and
troubles, and yet managed to make a fortune
ye told me.   Verily the ways of Providence
are mysterious."

I laughed somewhat harshly.   "I never
knew Providence concern itself about one's
money matters," I said, " but it is quite true
that I have had a somewhat adventurous life
and have managed to make, if not a fortune,
at least sufficient money to render me independent for the rest of my days.   Not that I
should ever care to be idle again."

"That's a good lad, that's a good lad,"
said the old man eagerly.   "Gold begets gold.
Use it well, don't be hurrying to spend it on
foolishness and extravagance.   Money is a
good thing and hard to get.   I never thought
you would be a rich man, Douglas, you were
aye careless and improvident."

" You wanted to put an old head on young
shoulders, sir," I said.   "That's not possible.
But let us not talk of myself any longer.
How are you, and how are folks here? . .

It seems as if I had been away long enough for many changes."

"I'm no hand at 'havers,'" he said abruptly. "I leave that for old women and young fools who think the world's only made for them to clatter about it Janet's weel and thriving you see, and as for myself, I'm no' so helpless but that I can walk to the town and back when I'm needing to do it."

"I am glad to hear it," I said, feeling a strange sense of compassion for the infirmity that vaunted its foolish economies, and the strange clinging to its idol of pelf even in the face of the approaching shadow which threatens all humanity. I talked to him for a short time longer, but we had never had much in common, and conversation was somewhat strained and difficult.

At last, on the plea of not liking to leave my friend longer alone and the long walk back to the town, I bade the old man good-night.

Just as I reached the door some lingering memory, some desire against which I had been battling uselessly all this night, prompted me to turn back and put one last question.

"By the way," I said, "what of the Camerons and the old lady at Craig Bank? Are they all well? I used to see a great deal of them, you know, when I was last here."

"I believe they're well enough," he said indifferently. "I'm not one to fash myself about my neighbours. I did hear Janet saying something about the old lady at Craig Bank. She was very ill this last winter, yet she's no more than my age, but women never wear so well as men folk. Her grandchild came to nurse her; the little lass that made the match wi' Campbell o' Corriemoor. That was a fine thing for her, and a proud day for the Camerons and Lindsays, I'm thinking. But I think the man must hae been daft myself to take up wi' a bit thing like yon. She'd neither sense, nor looks, nor tocher! Well, well, it's ill trying to teach other folks wisdom."

"But is Mrs. Lindsay better?" I asked eagerly.

"Better—well Janet says that'll never be this side o' the kirk-yard. I'm not sure but what the lassie is with her again. She came to the service a week back, I know, for I saw her myself."

I said no more, but my heart seemed to grow lighter of a long suffered weight. A strange comfort seemed to reach me through those careless words which for the speaker meant so little, for me so much.

Oh Athole! only once again to see you, to touch your hand, to hear your low sweet voice, and then——

Well, then, it seemed to me life might do its worst!

BOOK IV.

CHAPTER I.

" Tears, idle tears, I know not what they mean,
Tears from the depths of some divine despair
Rise in the heart, and gather to the eyes,
In looking on the happy Autumn fields,
And thinking of the days that are no more."

" THE greater part of life is made up of failures and mistakes."

I was reading that in a book the other day. The sentence has haunted me ever since. Is it true? If so how sad it sounds!

I am not of the opinion of the country-woman who said a certain aphorism must be true because she had seen it " in print," but I cannot help fancying that there must be some hidden meaning, some sad or bitter ex-perience of the writer's own life, underlying an expression that haunts one as one lays down the volume that contains it.

And all day, as I have looked across the wide moorland, or watched the sunlight on the glancing waters of the loch, and the clouds that change from grey to purple and gold, those words have bean ringing in my ears and sounding like a knell of doom in my heart.

For fully and frankly, and without disguise, I confess to myself that their truth has struck home, that my life is one of those made up of failures and mistakes. Or is it not rather one great failure, a record of that irrevocable mistake that again and again women have suffered for—a loveless and unsuitable marriage ?

If my unhappiness is of the passive order, yet none the less it is unhappiness. The sense of being in the wrong place, of utter want of sympathy with my surroundings, of absolute incapacity to interest myself in the domestic details that my mother-in-law finds so all-engrossing, or the farm news, and shooting and fishing triumphs of the Laird.

I have been married nearly two years and I am deadly sick of Corriemoor and its way of life. I know the plan of every day, I might almost say of every hour.

The few people who call on us, or with whom we exchange visits, are all it seems to me cut out on one pattern of conventionality. The men talk of their tenants or the prospects of the moors, with an occasional dash of politics or a religious controversy arising from some disputed text or point of doctrine, and drink copiously of whisky, the very sight and smell of which I loathe. The women discuss their household affairs, their neighbours and their doings, and patiently wait till their lords and masters have finished their libations, and are prepared to escort them to their respective abodes.

There are no young people with whom I can associate, nor does it seem to occur to Mrs. Campbell that I am quite out of my element with these dowagers and matrons.

They look upon me as a somewhat flighty and graceless person, and are fond of delivering lectures and counsels to which I listen with amusement or irritation according to my mood.

Only once have I been permitted to ask Bella to stay with me, and I think even her irrepressible spirits and bright geniality suffered under the general depression that reigned in the household. As the months drifted by and my little dead child was taken from me and laid in the desolate moorland churchyard, I grew more and more restless and unhappy. In vain I tried to assure myself that things would improve or that I should settle down into " my groove." They grew steadily worse.

My husband was kind, but he was not companionable, and certainly not observant. It never seemed to occur to him that I could possibly be dissatisfied with my life at Corrie-moor or find it anything but delightful. His mother had lived there ever since her married life began, and his grandfather's wife before

her, and another generation or two no doubt
ante-dated their advent. The young generation were expected to follow in the footsteps of those older and wiser members of
the family. I dared not say that the same-
ness and deadly dulness of the routine
were oppressing me to such a degree that
at times I was almost urged to outspoken
rebellion.

The weather too, was particularly dreary.
It rained incessantly throughout the summer,
and the disconsolate grey landscape, the
dripping trees, and the lowering sky, did not
form an inspiriting prospect, much as I had
heard about the never-failing beauty of
Corriemoor.

Perhaps the leaven of my own discontent
had entered into everything. But try as I
might, I could not make mind, feeling, tastes
and inclinations fit into the groove laid down
for them.

It needs the harsher discipline of life to
teach one patience and forbearance, but I was
young, passionate, enthusiastic, and therefore

fitted my surroundings about as well as the proverbial "peg" in its square hole.

I knew that there were people who would have been perfectly happy in my position, but I chafed like a restive steed under the perpetual restraint imposed on mind, word, and feeling.

I could not interest myself in my neigh-bours' concerns, though they were good enough to take an extraordinary interest in mine.

If one has any sense of the picturesque, the romantic, the dramatic, one cannot help trying to fit surroundings and associations accordingly. But my efforts were vain and my figures nothing but "lay-figures" of the very heaviest and prosiest type.

So in gloom and heaviness and depression the months dropped one by one into the lap of the past, and I was only aroused out of my long apathy by a sudden and terrifying summons from Grannie. She was dangerously ill—dying they said—and her one cry was for me.

The Laird took me to Inverness straight-way, and left me in the little hushed house that seemed so home-like and so dear.

Grannie was very ill, the doctor almost despaired of her, but she took "a turn" as they said very soon after my arrival, and in three weeks' time was convalescent. I stayed on. I was in no hurry to return to Corrie-moor and its gloom and loneliness.

At Craig Bank I felt at home. Some one or other of the Camerons were perpetually dropping in. Bella and I shared the duties of nursing between us. There was sunshine and air, exercise and pleasant companion-ship for me, and, as a flower expands and rejoices in a congenial atmosphere, so I grew brighter, happier, more content, and the change soon made itself apparent in my looks and manners and habits, as Bella speedily remarked.

"Such a queer bit creature," she said, in her merry, teazing way, "lifting its head like a flower after rain because it's petted and spoiled and fussed over! But what had they

done to you, Athole?" she added more
gravely, "you looked just broken down when
you came here. Aren't you happy, dearie?"

The old fond word, the old fond tones—
almost they broke me down. I shook my
head. "I'm as happy as I can expect to be,"
I said, "if there is a meaning to the word,
which I sometimes doubt. But my life is
very dull and depressing, Bella. That is the
honest truth."

"Well, they are rather old fogies for you,
my pet. I wish I were a bit nearer and
could run over and have a chat with you
every day."

"So do I," I echoed wearily, "my mother-
in-law and the Laird are not the liveliest
company in the world."

"But you have your books—your music?"
she said.

"They hate to see me reading, and they
only like me to play Scotch music," I answered gloomily. "Mrs. Campbell thinks I
ought to be always at needle-work, and you
know I detest it!"

"Yes, I know, she said with a humorous twinkle in her bright eyes. "I mind well the lazy wee lassie who would not put stitch or seam to gown for any coaxing; but as you're a rich fine lady now surely you have a maid to do your sewing."

"Oh, yes, but still Mrs. Campbell thinks I ought to do a good deal myself."

"But surely you are mistress, Athole, and can do what you like? You mustn't let the old lady rule you in everything."

"I'm afraid she's rather what you call a 'managing' person, Bella," I said ruefully. "I began by giving in to her and begging her to keep the position of mistress and she means to do so I can see."

Bella shook her head deprecatingly. "I told you that was a bad plan."

"But what could I do?" I urged. "I was too young and too ignorant to take my place as the head of the household. Besides, it would have been worse to have had her watching and criticising all my blunders. As it is, at least she has occupation, and I am

32*

saved the scoldings that I hear lavished on Jean, and Meg, and Janet perpetually."

"I'm afraid you're not quite happy, Athole?" she said gently.

I felt the tears rise to my eyes. "Oh, my dear," I said, "who in this world can expect to be that? There must always be a shadow to sunlight, a cross, a drawback, a want unsupplied. I am as well off as most people, better perhaps than many. I ought not to be discontented. The pebble in my shoe is a very small one."

"But there should be no pebble at all," she said. "Even a small one makes its sore, when the journey is long."

"Perhaps," I said drearily, "my journey may not be very long. Sometimes I pray so."

She turned away somewhat abruptly. For that night we talked no more of Corriemoor, or my life there.

*   *   *   *   *

Grannie's health steadily improved and the Laird's letters began to suggest my return. I was in no hurry to notice his hints, I felt a growing disinclination to go back to the prison-house I loathed, after this unexpected spell of liberty. Bella, I fear, somewhat encouraged my insubordination. We were so happy together; we had such innocent jests and jokes, such long delicious walks, such tender half-spoken confidences.

Kenneth came up from Edinburgh for a week. I had not seen him since I married. He was very much altered, grave, reticent, self-important. He had given himself up heart and soul to his studies and profession, and was everywhere spoken of with the Scotch measure of cautious praise as "likely to do well."

We did not get on at all, he and I. I disliked the masterful importance of his newly-acquired manner, and he, to all intents and purposes, had not approved of my marriage and was fond of making disparaging remarks concerning the Laird, and affairs at Corrie-moor generally. I was not sorry when he left. I had but four days more of liberty and

then I must leave Craig Bank. An impera-
tive summons had reached me and I knew
excuses could no longer avail.

One afternoon I had left Grannie asleep,
and was hurrying along the High Street on
my way to the Camerons'.

It was a dull misty day, with lowering sky
that threatened rain, and a piercing easterly
wind that made me draw my warm cloak
closely round me as I walked along.

The street was almost deserted. I saw but
two figures in the whole length of the
thoroughfare. They were approaching me
from the opposite direction.

Suddenly something in the walk, height,
bearing of one of them struck me as familiar.
My heart gave one quick leap—the blood
seemed to rush in a burning torrent to my
face—my feet refused to stir.

Were not the seas between us? Had we
not said good-bye for ever? Yet surely fancy
was playing me no trick now.

Dizzily, stupidly, I tried to collect my wits
—to pass on quietly and unconcernedly, with

but one glance that seemed rather to defy than to court recognition.

In vain. A start, a husky cry—the cry of an emotion strong and swift as pain and sorrow and memory could make it, and then —my hand was clasped in the warm, strong clasp of old, and once more I stood pale and trembling in the presence of Douglas Hay!

CHAPTER II.

"We twain shall not remeasure
The ways that left us twain."

Two years—two years of trial, suffering, weariness—rolled back as a scroll before flame. My heart, that had so long forgotten to feel glad, fluttered like a bird at sound of that voice speaking my name—the blood that had known no change in its even flow, coutsed madly and wildly through my veins as once again I met those eyes that had been the only lover's eyes to me.

What mattered that we had parted in anger? What mattered bitterness, pride, distrust, coldness? One unguarded moment had bereft me of all composure, and I stood face to face with just the one being in the world who had the power to so move and discompose me—truth speaking out in face and eyes, and trembling voice — truth that defied all effort at coldness.

He was equally agitated. The colour faded from his face, his eyes spoke of pain and gladness both, the hand that clasped mine trembled like a weak girl's, the very accents of his voice were unsteady.

With a strong effort I regained my self-control. I saw the keen eyes of the stranger, who was with Douglas, watching us both intently.

I expressed surprise at seeing him back in Scotland. For two years no word of him had reached me—I imagined he was still in Canada.

" But I have never been to Canada at all," he said. " Is it possible you did not hear that I was shipwrecked ? "

" I have heard nothing," I answered simply, "I live so far away—and news travels slowly——"

"True—I—I forgot," he said huskily. "Your home is at Corriemoor. Are you staying long in Inverness ? "

"Three days more," I said quietly. "Grannie has been very ill and she sent for me to come here. I have been at Craig Bank for the last six weeks. When did you arrive?"

"Only yesterday," he said, and then opportunely remembering his companion, he introduced him to me by the name of "Mr. Huel Penryth."

A strange name, I thought, and a strange man too. My first impression of him was not favourable. The face was a powerful one, but stern and cold, with dark inscrutable eyes that read more than they revealed. The wild thick hair, streaked with grey, fell back from a broad and heavily-lined brow. Care and suffering and endurance had left their mark upon this man. So much even my inexperienced eye could tell.

He raised his hat with grave politeness, as I bowed in answer to Douglas's hurried murmur, and as I met his glance it seemed to me that he had read my secret, and was speculating as to its future bearing on my

life. I could not have explained why I felt
this, but the consciousness was so acute that I
could almost have fancied it had flashed from
brain to brain, as the electric current flies
from one centre of active force to another.

He spoke, and his voice held a charm that
could not be gainsaid. Full, rich, and with
a melancholy sweetness of intonation—I
found myself listening to the sound even more
than to the words. And they were not mere
conventional words either.

They briefly conveyed the history of that
shipwreck and the friendship that had been
born of mutual hardship, endurance and
companionship. It was the history of those
two blank years summed up and presented
to me with an elaborate simplicity that yet
seemed to lack no detail.

Douglas showed signs of impatience.
"Where are you bound for?" he asked at
last. "We are keeping you standing in the
cold all this time."

I mentioned my destination, and they both
turned and walked with me.

How strange it seemed — how strange I
felt. I was as one in dreamland—haunted
by past visions that were floating and centre-
ing themselves in the present. A word, a
glance, a smile, and how much was said and
recalled.

Timidly I glanced at Douglas's face from
time to time.

How altered it was. All the boyishness
and youth had fled. It was stern and grave,
and had lost much of the bright colouring
and animation that had lent it so great a
charm. But instinctively I felt that it had
gained in experience and character far more
than it had lost of youth and gaiety.

We met on very different ground to that
on which we had parted, yet I think the
memory of that parting was keenly with us
both. I had been so hard and unforgiving—
he so sad and so remorseful. But all was
altered now. We were boy and girl no
longer. Life had grown of interest and importance to him, and had surrounded me
with duties and responsibilities. Yet it was

hard to put the new personality in place of the old. To see only Mrs. Campbell of Corriemoor, in the Athole Lindsay of both our memories.

I noticed he never addressed me by my married name. I felt inclined to ask him when and how he had heard of that event, but somehow I could not frame the words, and I therefore talked, or tried to talk, of more conventional matters connected with mutual friends and mutual interests.

We reached the Camerons' house and I paused at the gate.

"I shall call on them in the course of a day or two," said Douglas. "Not this morning. Do you think," he added hesitatingly, "that Mrs. Lindsay would be well enough to see me if I paid her a visit?"

"She would be very pleased, I am sure," I answered. "She comes downstairs now every afternoon."

Then we shook hands once more, and they turned down the street, while I went into Aunt Cameron's domicile.

The girls were round me in a moment. brimful of eager curiosity. They had seen me and my two companions from the window.

Was that really—surely it could not be Douglas Hay? How old and altered he was — how tall he looked — and who was his friend?—and so on, and so on.

Their merry chatter, their incessant questioning jarred on me at times, but I did my best to satisfy their curiosity, adding that Douglas Hay himself would be round to see them in a day or two.

After a while the younger girls drifted away to their usual duties or occupations. Bella and I were alone.

There was a space of silence, then her bright dark eyes met mine with grave scrutiny.

"How did you feel?" she asked abruptly. "It was rather—unexpected."

"That," I said, with a faint laugh, "was just what I felt. You could not have expressed it better."

"And you don't mind? You can be friends?" she persisted. "I am rather sorry he came here. What brought him?"

"Natural affection, no doubt," I said. "He came to see his father!"

"Of course he had heard of your marriage! Who told him?"

"He mentioned Corriemoor as my place of abode," I said. "But I did not ask who was his informant."

She was silent for a moment. Then she came to me, quite suddenly, and folded her arms about me and drew me to her dear true heart.

"Oh, my dearie," she said, "don't speak in that hard, cold way to me. Have I not known it all—have I not seen you fighting your battle month by month, year by year? And hasn't it wrung my heart again and again to watch the change in your wee face, that has grown so sad and weariful of late? But I'd be no true friend to you, Athole, if I did not speak the plain truth now. There is far more danger in your meeting with

Douglas Hay than ever there was before. It is wiser to recognize a temptation than to believe in one's power of resistance when the danger comes. You will promise me not to see him or meet him, won't you, dear? You'll only be laying up fresh unhappiness for yourself if you do. Mind, I speak plainly. It is not as if your marriage had contented you, and he will watch that very keenly and—if he still cares——"

"Oh, Bella—but that is all over long—long ago," I interrupted.

"Love is a hard thing to kill," she said. "There is just one final ending to it, but neither you nor he touched that."

"I think," I said, coldly, "there is nothing to fear now Bella, not on either side. Even if there were—well I am here but three days more—after that I shall probably never see him again."

"I hope so," she said earnestly. "I hope it all the more because I know how useless are warnings, counsels, efforts, in a case like this. I never had a high opinion of Douglas

Hay's character, as you know, but that does not prevent my seeing he is very attractive and very fascinating."

"That," I said, "could never touch me again—nothing in that way—I want something deep, real, strong. Something to lean on and depend on—I suppose," I added with a little bitterness, " it sounds very shocking to say such a thing, but I should like to have liberty to experiment on different people and see how they affect me, or I them. It seems as if life hampered us so dreadfully we can't really *know* each other. We can't say what our real feelings or natures are unless they are tested. I seem to know people so little, and yet I always want to get below the surface, to touch something that will respond and answer to my own appeal, my own needs. But I never can— I never can."

She was silent. Presently she said, " That is an odd fancy on your part, Athole, I don't wonder you are unhappy. You ask too much of life, and feel too deeply."

"Perhaps that is so," I answered. "I am not happy, I am not contented, and I am not good. Yet I might be all, and I long to be very often. I wonder where the secret of my failure lies? In myself, of course, but how can I comprehend or reach it? One's inner nature is always more or less of a mystery. When I think of what I am and what I want — of the intense longings for a fuller and deeper life — the perpetual rebellion against my groove, I feel tempted to do something desperate. I only act and re-act upon myself. No wonder I feel storm-beaten."

"It seems strange to look at you and then hear you talk like this," said Bella thoughtfully. "If your life was more active you would be less morbid."

"My life is destined to be always as it is now, I fear," I answered, drawing away from her arms at last. "It is my only comfort to have you to talk to, Bella. I think no one else understands me — or — or cares very much."

" Your husband cares for you, dearie. He is grave and serious, and perhaps he seems cold, but he is so good."

" Oh, I know that," I answered. " It is my own ceaseless reproach. Sometimes I think I must be very ungrateful, very wicked, but I can't help it. I can't alter myself as I said before. If I could——"

" Well?" she said, looking at me gravely with a little troubled pucker of her white smooth brow.

" Oh," I said laughing. " I would turn myself into Meg or Jean, of course, with no thought beyond the ' kye at the byrne ' and the stocking-knitting for the household. How I envy the dull common-place content of such lives ! "

" I'm sure you don't — not really," said Bella with energy. " But my opinion is you want rousing—change. Why can't you get the Laird to take you away ? He went abroad once and he told me he enjoyed it very much, why shouldn't he go again ? "

I laughed as I remembered some passages

of that foreign tour, and the passive composure and grim endurance which Donald had displayed.

"If he told you so," I answered, "be very sure he did not mean it. He hates foreign travel and foreign ways ; even foreign scenery could only bring a reluctant admission from his lips that it was 'no that bad.' I believe he thinks Nature quite incapable of favouring any land but Scotland. Oh, dear," I added with a sigh, "how hard it is to be fettered and hampered like this — to be a prisoner with one's chains always weighing one down. Now if only you and I could go off together, Bella, that would be some fun, wouldn't it? And though there's no reason why we shouldn't, yet picture to yourself the outcry that would arise at the bare suggestion. How all our Scotch Mrs. Grundys would hold up their hands in righteous horror at the 'impropriety.' Oh! how I envy American girls. They do get some enjoyment out of life and youth. And I'm sure they're not a bit the worse for it."

"I never met one," said Bella with a gravity that set me off laughing. "But they're rather bold and forward, are they not?"

"I never found them so, and I've come across plenty in my travels," I said. "Very free and independent, if you like, and as a rule far better educated than English girls. At least they talk better and seem to be at home on most subjects. They are far more brilliant and amusing than girls of any other nation."

"But not nearly so refined and well-bred," argued Bella.

I shrugged my shoulders.

"That means not so dull or depressed, or conventional! Of course their manners and habits are very different to ours, but I always found them interesting."

"Well," said Bella, laughing. "I almost wish we could turn ourselves into American girls for the time being, and go off on a foreign tour, as you suggest. I've always been crazy to go abroad, but I might as

well ask for the moon as for permission
to do it, or opportunity even if I had the
permission."

"Well, I must go back now," I said with a
sigh. "Come round this evening, Bella, if
you've nothing to do. It's so dull when
Grannie goes to bed."

"Certainly, I'll come," she said briskly.
"Must you really go back to Corriemoor on
Saturday ? "

"No help for it," I answered. "But I
really do not see why I shouldn't take you
back with me, dear."

"Mrs. Campbell doesn't like me," she said
laughing. "I'm not staid enough, or grave
enough, I fancy."

"Never mind Mrs. Campbell," I said.
"Surely I may be permitted a little independence. The Laird is coming here for
me, I'll tell him you'll return and stay a few
weeks with us. May I ? "

"Now, Athole, you know well I'm always
happy to be with you, but——"

"No buts—no buts!" I cried putting my

hands to my ears. "I'll settle all the 'pros and cons' and you pack your box. You needn't be particular; anything does for Corriemoor!"

END OF VOL. II

PRINTED BY
KELLY AND CO., GATE STREET, LINCOLN'S INN FIELDS, W.C
AND KINGSTON-ON-THAMES.